Siri Hustvedt

Siri Hustvedt's first novel, *The Blindfold*, was published by Sceptre in 1993 and her second, *The Enchantment of Lily Dahl*, followed in 1997. Her third novel, *What I Loved*, was published in 2003 to great acclaim and was an international bestseller. It was followed in 2009 by *The Sorrows of an American*. She is also the author of *Reading to You*, a poetry collection, and three collections of essays, *Yonder, Mysteries of the Rectangle: Essays on Painting*, and *A Plea for Eros*. She lives in Brooklyn, New York, with her husband Paul Auster.

Siri Hustvedt

The Blindfold

SCEPTRE

First published in Great Britain in 1993 by Sceptre
An imprint of Hodder & Stoughton
An Hachette UK company

First published in paperback in 1994

21

A CIP catalogue record for this title is available from the British Library.

ISBN 978 0 340 58123 0

Typeset in Sabon by Palimpsest Book Production Limited,
Grangemouth, Stirlingshire

Printed and bound by CPI Group (UK) Ltd, Croydon, CR0 4YY

Hodder & Stoughton policy is to use papers that are natural, renewable and
recyclable products and made from wood grown in sustainable forests. The
logging and manufacturing processes are expected to conform to the
environmental regulations of the country of origin.

Hodder & Stoughton Ltd
338 Euston Road
London NW1 3BH

www.hodder.co.uk

For Paul Auster

ONE

Sometimes even now I think I see him in the street or standing in a window or bent over a book in a coffee shop. And in that instant, before I understand that it's someone else, my lungs tighten and I lose my breath.

I met him eight years ago. I was a graduate student then at Columbia University. It was hot that summer and my nights were often sleepless. I lay awake in my two-room apartment on West 109th Street listening to the city's noises. I would read, write, and smoke into the morning, but on some nights when the heat made me too listless to work, I watched the neighbors from my bed. Through my barred window, across the narrow airshaft, I looked into the apartment opposite mine and saw the two men who lived there wander from one room to another, half dressed in the sultry weather. On a day in July, not long before I met Mr. Morning, one of the men came naked to the window. It was dusk and he stood there for a long time, his body lit from behind by a yellow lamp. I hid in the darkness of my bedroom and he never knew I was there. That was two months after Stephen left me, and I thought of him incessantly, stirring in the humid sheets, never comfortable, never relieved.

During the day, I looked for work. In June I had done research for a medical historian. Five days a week I sat in the reading room at the Academy of Medicine on East 103rd Street, filling up index cards with information about great diseases—bubonic plague, leprosy, influenza, syphilis, tuberculosis—as well as more obscure afflictions that I remember now only because of their names—yaws, milk leg, greensickness, ragsorter's disease, housemaid's knee, and dandy fever. Dr. Rosenberg, an octogenarian who spoke and moved very slowly, paid me six dollars an hour to fill up those index cards, and although I never understood what he did with them, I never asked him, fearing that an explanation might take hours. The job ended when my employer went to Italy. I had always been poor as a student, but Dr. Rosenberg's vacation made me desperate. I hadn't paid the July rent, and I had no money for August. Every day, I went to the bulletin board in Philosophy Hall where jobs were posted, but by the time I called, they had always been taken. Nevertheless, that was how I found Mr. Morning. A small handwritten notice announced the position: "Wanted. Research assistant for project already under way. Student of literature preferred. Herbert B. Morning." A phone number appeared under the name, and I called immediately. Before I could properly introduce myself, a man with a beautiful voice gave me an address on Amsterdam Avenue and told me to come over as soon as possible.

It was hazy that day, but the sun glared and I blinked in the light as I walked through the door of Mr. Morning's tenement building. The elevator was broken, and I remember sweating while I climbed the stairs to the fourth floor. I can still see his intent face in the doorway. He was a very pale man with a large, handsome nose. He breathed loudly as he opened the door and let me into a tiny, stifling room that smelled of cat. The walls were lined with stuffed bookshelves, and more books were piled in leaning towers all over the room. There were tall stacks of newspapers and magazines as well, and beneath a window whose blinds had been tightly shut was a heap of old clothes or rags. A massive wooden desk stood in the center of the room, and on it were perhaps a dozen boxes of various sizes. Close to the desk was a narrow bed, its rumpled sheets strewn with more books. Mr. Morning seated himself behind the desk, and I sat down in an old folding chair across from him. A narrow ray of light that had escaped through a broken blind fell to the floor between us, and when I looked at it, I saw a haze of dust.

I smoked, contributing to the room's blur, and looked at the skin of his neck; it was moon white. He told me he was happy I had come and then fell silent. Without any apparent reserve, he looked at me, taking in my whole body with his gaze. I don't know if his scrutiny was lecherous or merely curious, but I felt assaulted and turned away from him, and then when he asked me my name, I lied. I did it quickly, without hesitation, inventing a new patronym: Davidsen. I became Iris Davidsen. It was a defensive act, a way of protecting myself from some amorphous danger, but later that false name haunted me; it seemed to move me elsewhere, shifting me off course and strangely altering my whole world for a time. When I think back on it now, I imagine that lie as the beginning of the story, as a kind of door to my uneasiness. Everything else I told him was true—about my parents and sisters in Minnesota, about my studies in nineteenth-century English literature, my past research jobs, even my telephone number. As I talked, he smiled at me, and I thought to myself, It's an intimate smile, as if he has known me for years.

He told me that he was a writer, that he wrote for magazines to earn money. "I write about everything for every taste," he said. "I've written for *Field and Stream*, *House and Garden*, *True Confessions*, *True Detective*, *Reader's Digest*. I've written stories, one spy novel, poems, essays, reviews—I even did an art catalog once." He grinned and waved an arm. " 'Stanley Rubin's rhythmical canvases reveal a debt to Mannerism—Pontormo in particular. The long, undulating shapes hint at . . .' " He laughed. "And I rarely publish under the same name."

"Don't you stand behind what you write?"

"I am behind everything I write, Miss Davidsen, usually sitting, sometimes standing. In the eighteenth century, it was common to stand and write—at an escritoire. Thomas Wolfe wrote standing."

"That's not exactly what I meant."

"No, of course it isn't. But you see, Herbert B. Morning couldn't possibly write for *True Confessions*, but Fern Luce can. It's as simple as that."

"You enjoy hiding behind masks?"

"I revel in it. It gives my life a certain color and danger."

"Isn't danger overstating it a bit?"

"I don't think so. Nothing is beyond me as long as I adopt the correct name for each project. It isn't arbitrary. It requires a gift, a genius, if I may say so myself, for hitting on the alias that will unleash the right man or woman for the job. Dewitt L. Parker wrote that art catalog, for example, and Martin Blane did the spy novel. But there are risks, too. Even the most careful planning can go awry. It's impossible to know for sure who's concealed under the pseudonym I choose."

"I see," I said. "In that case, I should probably ask you who you are now."

"You have the privilege, dear lady, of addressing Herbert

B. Morning himself, unencumbered by any other person-
alities."

"And what does Mr. Morning need a research assistant
for?"

"For a kind of biography," he said. "For a project about
life's paraphernalia, is bits and pieces, treasures and refuse.
I need someone like you to respond freely to the objects
in question. I need an ear and an eye, a scribe and a voice,
a Friday for every day of the week, someone who is sharp,
sensitive. You see, I'm in the process of prying open the
very essence of the inanimate world. You might say that
it's an anthropology of the present."

I asked him to be more specific about the job.

"It began three years ago when she died." He paused as
if thinking. "A girl—a young woman. I knew her, but not
very well. Anyway, after she died, I found myself in possession of a number of her things, just common everyday
things. I had them in the apartment, this and that, out and
about, objects that were lost, abandoned, speechless, but
not dead. That was the crux of it. They weren't dead, not
in the usual way we think of objects as lifeless. They seemed
charged with a kind of power. At times I almost felt them
move with it, and then after several weeks, I noticed that
they seemed to lose that vivacity, seemed to retreat into
their thingness. So I boxed them."

"You boxed them?" I said.

"I boxed them to keep them untouched by the here and
now. I feel sure that those things carry her imprint—the
mark of a warm, living body on the world. And even though
I've tried to keep them safe, they're turning cold. I can tell.
It's been too long, so my work is urgent. I have to act
quickly. I'll pay you sixty dollars per object."

"Per object?" I was sweating in the chair and adjusted my position, pulling my skirt down under my legs, which felt strangely cool to the touch.

"I'll explain everything," he said. He took a small tape recorder from a drawer in his desk and pushed it toward me. "Listen to this first. It will tell you most of what you want to know. While you listen, I'll leave the room." He stood up from his chair and walked to a door. A large yellow cat appeared from behind a box and followed him. "Press play," he commanded, and vanished.

When I reached for the machine, I noticed two words scrawled on a legal pad near it: "woman's hand." The words seemed important, and I remember them as if they were the passwords to an underground life. When I turned on the tape, a woman's voice whispered, "This belonged to the deceased. It is a white sheet for a single bed . . ." What followed was a painstaking description of the sheet. It included every tiny discoloration and stain, the texture of the aged cotton, and even the tag from which the words had disappeared in repeated washings. It lasted for perhaps ten minutes; the entire speech was delivered in that peculiar half-voice. The description itself was tedious and yet I listened with anticipation, imagining that the words would soon reveal something other than the sheet. They didn't. When the tape ended, I looked over to the door behind which Mr. Morning had hidden and saw that it was now ajar and half of his face was pressed through the opening. He was lit from behind, and I couldn't see his features clearly, but the pale hair on his head was shining, and again I heard him breathe with difficulty as he walked toward me. He reached out for my hand. Without thinking, I withdrew it.

"You want descriptions of that girl's things, is that it?" I could hear the tightness and formality in my voice. "I don't understand what a recorded description has to do with your project as a whole or why the woman on the tape was whispering."

"The whisper is essential, because the full human voice is too idiosyncratic, too marked with its own history. I'm looking for anonymity so the purity of the object won't be blocked from coming through, from displaying itself in its nakedness. A whisper has no character."

The project seemed odd to the point of madness, but I was drawn to it. Chance had given me this small adventure and I was pleased. I also felt that beneath their eccentricity, Mr. Morning's ideas had a weird kind of logic. His comments about whispering, for example, made sense.

"Why don't you write out the descriptions?" I said. "Then there will be no voice at all to interfere with the anonymity you want." I watched his face closely.

He leaned over the desk and looked directly at me. "Because," he said, "then there's no living presence, no force to prompt an awakening."

I shifted in my chair again, gazing at the pile of rags under the window. "What do you mean by awakening?"

"I mean that the objects in question begin to stir under scrutiny, that they, mute as they are, can nevertheless bear witness to human mysteries."

"You mean they're clues to this girl's life? You want to know about her, is that it? Aren't there more direct routes for finding out biographical information?"

"Not the kind of biography I'm interested in." He smiled at me, this time opening his mouth, and I admired his large white teeth. He isn't old, I thought, not even fifty.

He leaned over and picked up a blue box from the floor—
a medium-sized department store box—and handed it to
me.

I pulled at its lid.

"Not now!" He almost cried out. "Not here."

I pushed the lid back down.

"Do it at home alone. The object must be kept wrapped
and in the box unless you are working. Study it. Describe
it. Let it speak to you. I have a recorder and a new tape
for you as well. Oh yes, and you should begin your description with the words, 'This belonged to the deceased.'
Could you have it for me by the day after tomorrow?"

I told him I could and then left the apartment with my
box and tape recorder, rushing out into the daylight. I
walked quickly away from the building and didn't look
into the box until I had turned the corner and was sure
that he couldn't see me from his window. Inside was a
rather dirty white glove lying on a bed of tissue paper.

I didn't go home until later. I fled the heat by going into
an air-conditioned coffee shop, sitting for hours as I scrib-
bled notes to myself about the glove and made calculations
as to the number of objects I needed to describe before I
could pay my rent. I imagined my descriptions as pithy,
elegant compositions, small literary exercises based on a
kind of belated nineteenth-century positivism. Just for the
moment, I decided to pretend that the thing really can be
captured by the word. I drank coffee, ate a glazed dough-
nut, and was happy.

But that night when I put the glove beside my typewriter

to begin work, it seemed to have changed. I felt it, felt the lumpy wool, and then very slowly pulled it over my left hand. It was too small for my long fingers and didn't cover my wrist. As I looked at it, I had the uncanny feeling that I had seen the same glove on another hand. I began to tug abruptly at its fingers, until it sailed to the floor. I let it lie there for several minutes, unwilling to touch it. The small woolen hand covered with smudges and snags seemed terrible to me, a stranded and empty thing, both non-sensical and cruel. Finally I snatched it up and threw it back into the box. There would be no writing until the next day. It was too hot; I was too tired, too nervous. I lay in bed near the open window, but the air stood still. I touched my clammy skin and looked over at the opposite apartment, but the two men had gone to sleep and their windows were black. Before I slept I moved the box into the other room.

That night the screaming began. I woke to the noise but couldn't identify it and thought at first that it was the demented howling of cats I had heard earlier in the sum-mer. But it was a woman's voice—a long, guttural wail that ended in a growl. "Stop it! I hate you! I hate you!" she screamed over and over. I stiffened to the noise and wondered if I should call the police, but for a long time I just waited and listened. Someone yelled "Shut up!" from a window and it stopped. I expected it to begin again, but it was over. I wet a washcloth with cold water and rubbed my neck, arms, and face with it. I thought of Stephen then, as I had often seen him, at his desk, his head turned slightly away from me, his large eyes looking down at a paper. That was when his body was still enchanted; it had a power that I battled and raged against for months. Later that enchantment fell away, and he passed into a banality I never would have thought possible.

The next morning I began again. By daylight the box on the kitchen table had returned to its former innocence. Using my notes from the coffee shop, I worked steadily, but it was difficult. I looked at the glove closely, trying to remember the words for its various parts, for its texture and the color of its stains. I noticed that the tip of the index finger was blackened, as if the owner had trailed her finger along a filthy surface. She was probably left-handed, I thought; that's a gesture for the favored hand. A girl running her finger along a subway railing. The image prompted a shudder of memory: "woman's hand." The words may have referred to her hand, her gloved hand, or to the glove itself. The connection seemed rife with meaning, and yet it spawned nothing inside me but a feeling akin to guilt. I pressed on with the description, but the more I wrote, the more specific I was about the glove's characteristics, the more remote it became. Rather than fixing it in the light of scientific exactitude, the abundance of detail made the glove disappear. In fact, my minute description of its discolorations, snags, and pills, its loosened threads and stretched palm seemed alien to the sad little thing before me.

In the evening I edited my work and then read it into the machine. Whispering bothered me; it made the words clandestine, foreign, and when I listened to the tape, I didn't recognize my own voice. It sounded like a precocious child lisping absurdities from some invisible part of the room, and when I heard it, I blushed with a shame I still don't understand.

Late that night I woke to the screaming again, but it stopped after several minutes, just as before. This time I couldn't get back to sleep and lay awake for hours in a vague torment as the shattered images of exhaustion and heat crowded my brain.

Mr. Morning didn't answer the bell right away. I pressed it three times and was about to leave when I heard him shuffling to the door. He paused in the doorway, looked me directly in the eyes, and smiled. The beautiful smile startled me, and I turned away from him. He apologized for the delay but gave no explanation. That day the apartment seemed more chaotic than on my first visit; the desk in particular was a mass of disturbed papers and boxes. He asked me for the tape; I gave it to him, and then he ushered me from the room, gently pushing me behind the door where he had concealed himself the last time.

I found myself in the kitchen, a tiny room, even hotter and smellier than the other. There were a few unwashed dishes in the sink, several books piled on the counter, and one large, white box. From the next room I could just manage to hear the sound of the tape and my soft voice droning on about the glove. I paged through a couple of books—a world atlas and a little copy of *The Cloud of Unknowing*—but I was really interested in the box. I stood over it. The corners of the lid were worn, as if it had been opened many times; two of the sides were taped shut. I ran my finger over the tape to see if I could loosen it. I picked at the tape's yellow skin with my nail, but my efforts made it pucker and tear, so I stopped, trying again on the other side. My head was bent over the box when I heard him coming toward the door, and I leapt backward, accidentally pushing the box off the counter. It fell to the floor but didn't open. I was able to return it to its place before Mr. Morning appeared in the doorway. Whether or not he saw my hands dart away from the box, I still don't know, but when the box fell, whatever was inside it made a loud, hollow, rattling noise, and he must have heard that. Yet he said nothing.

We walked into the other room and sat down. He looked at me and I remember thinking that his gaze had a peculiar strength and that he seemed to blink less often than most people.

"Was the tape okay?" I asked.

"Fine," he said, "but there was one aspect of the thing you neglected to describe and I think it's rather important."

"What's that?"

"The odor."

"I didn't think of it," I said.

"No," he said, "many people don't, but without its smell, a thing loses its identity; the absence of odor cripples your description, makes it two-dimensional. Every object has its own scent and carries the odor of its place as well. This can be invaluable to an investigation."

"How?" I said it loudly.

He paused and looked at the window. "By evoking something crucial, something unnoticed before, a place or time or word. Just think of the things we forget in closets and attics, the mildew, the dust, the crushed dry bodies of insects—these odors leave their traces. My mother's trunks smelled of wet wool and lavender. It took me a long time to realize what that odor was, but then I identified it, and I remembered events I had forgotten."

"Is there something you want to remember about this girl who died?" I asked.

"Why do you say that?" He jerked his head toward me.

"Because you obviously want something out of all this. You want these descriptions for a reason. When you mentioned those trunks, I thought you might want to trigger a memory."

He looked away again. "A memory of a whole world," he said.

"But I thought you hardly knew her, Mr. Morning."

He picked up a pencil and began to doodle on a notebook page. "Did I tell you that?"

"Yes, you did."

"It's true. I didn't know her well."

"What is it you're after, then? Who was this person you're investigating?"

"I would like to know that too."

"You're evading my questions. She had a name, didn't she, this girl?"

"Her name won't help you, Miss Davidsen." His voice was nearly a whisper.

"Well, it won't hurt me either," I said.

He continued to move the pencil idly on the page in front of him. I craned to see it, trying to disguise the gesture by adjusting my skirt. There were several letters written on the paper—what looked like an *I*, a *Y*, a *B*, an *O*, an *M*, and a *D*. He had circled the *M*. If those markings were intended to form some kind of order, it was impossible to make it out, but even then, before I suspected anything, those letters had a strange effect on me. They stayed with me like the small but persistent aches of a mild illness.

Putting the pencil down, he looked up at me and nodded. He patted his chest. "The heat has given you a rash—here."

"No, it's my birthmark." I touched the skin just below my collarbone.

"A port-wine stain," he said. "It has character—a mark for life. If you'll forgive me for saying so, I've always found flaws like that poignant, little outward signs of our mortality. I used a birthmark in something I wrote once—"

I interrupted him. "You aren't going to tell me anything, are you?"

"You're referring to our subject, I take it?"

"Of course."

"I think you've failed to understand the nature of your task. I hired you precisely because you know nothing. I hired you to see what I cannot see, because you are who you are. I don't pretend that you're a blank slate. You bring your life with you, your nineteenth-century novels, your Minnesota, the fullness of your existence in every respect, but you didn't know her. When you look at the things I give you, when you write and then speak about them, your words and voice may be the catalysts of some undiscovered being. Knowledge of her will only distract you from your work. Let us say, for the sake of an example, that her name was Allison Hart and that she died of leukemia. Something appears before you, an image. A row of hospital beds perhaps, in a large room lit by those fluorescent tubes, and you see her, I'm sure you do. Allison—it's a romantic name—pale and emaciated, once beautiful, she lies under white sheets . . . And what you see will not only be shaped by my words but by my inflections, my expression, and then you will lose your freedom."

I began to speak, but he stopped me.

"No, let me say my piece. Let us say I tell you that her name was"—he paused—"Maxine Robinson and that she was murdered." He looked out past me toward the door and squinted as if he were trying to see something far away. He took several deep breaths. "That she was killed right here in this building. What would you compose then, Miss Davidsen, when you look inside my boxes? You'd be suffocated by what you know, just as I am. It wouldn't do; it just wouldn't do."

"You're playing with me and I resent it," I said. "If you admit that I bring my own associations to the descriptions, why shouldn't I bring my own baggage to the facts of her life? And death."

"Because!" he almost shouted. "Because we are about the business of discovery, of resurrection, not burial." He grabbed the edge of the desk and shook it. "Atonement, Miss Davidsen. Atonement!"

"Good God," I said, "atonement for what?"

He was suddenly calm. He pushed his chair back, crossed his legs, folded his arms, and cocked his head to one side. These movements seemed self-conscious, almost theatrical. "For the sins of the world."

"What does that mean?"

"It means exactly what the words denote."

"Those words, Mr. Morning," I said, "are liturgical. You've gone into a religious mode all of a sudden. What am I to think? You seem to have a talent for saying nothing with style."

"Be patient, and I think you'll begin to understand me." He was smiling.

I had no reply for him. The hot room, the darkness, his outburst and incomprehensible speech, had robbed me of the will to answer. Exhaustion had come over me in a matter of seconds. My bones hurt. Finally I said, "I should leave now."

"If you stay, I'll make tea for you. I'll feed you crumpets and tell you stories. I'll dazzle you with my impeccable manners, my wit and imagination."

I shook my head. "I really have to go."

He paid me with three twenty-dollar bills and gave me another box—this time a small white jeweler's box. He told me he didn't need the description until Monday of the following week. I had four days. We shook hands and then just before I walked through the door, he patted my arm. It was a gesture of sympathy and I accepted it as if it were owed to me.

Inside the second box was a stained and misshapen cotton ball. I found myself hesitant to touch it, as though it were contaminated. The wad of fiber was colored with makeup or powder that looked orange in the light and was also marked with an unidentifiable clot of something dense and brown. I drew away from the little box. Had he salvaged this thing after her death? I imagined him in a bathroom bending over a wastebasket to retrieve the used cotton ball. How had he found these things? Had he hoarded more of her refuse in boxes? I saw him alone, his fingers tracing the outlines of an object as he sat in his chair in front of the window with the closed blinds. But in the daydream I couldn't see what he held. I saw only his body hunched over it.

In those four days between visits to Mr. Morning, I was never free of him. Bits and pieces of his conversation invaded my thoughts, appearing unsummoned at all hours, especially at night. The idea that the girl had been murdered in his building took hold of me, and I began to imagine it. He had taunted me with it; he had intended to entice me with it as just another possible death, but once it was said, I felt that I had known it from the beginning. Resurrection. Atonement. He had seemed genuinely passionate. I remembered his troubled breathing as he spoke, the letters on the page, the white box falling, his hand on my arm. At the same time, I told myself that the man was a charlatan, someone who loved games, riddles, innuendo. Nothing he said could be believed. But in the end it was his posing that made me suspect that he had hidden the truth among his lies and that he was earnest about his project and the girl.

That night I worked for hours on the description. I held the cotton ball with a pair of tweezers up to the light, trying to find words that would express it, but the thing was lost to language; it resisted it even more than the glove. And when I tried metaphors, the object sank so completely into the other thing that I abandoned making comparisons. What was this piece of waste? As I sat sniffing the fibers and poking at the brown stain with a needle, I was overwhelmed by a feeling of disgust. The cotton ball told me nothing. It was a blank, a cipher; it probably had no connection to anything terrible, and yet I felt as if I had intruded on a shameful secret, that I had seen what I should not have seen. I composed slowly and my mind wandered. It was a night of many sounds: a man and a woman were fighting in Spanish next door; fire sirens howled and I heard a miserable dog crying somewhere close. At around two o'clock, in the baking confines of my bedroom, I whis-

pered the description into the machine. After it was recorded, I put the cotton ball back into its box and hid it
and the tape inside a cupboard in the other room. As I
shut the door I realized I was behaving like a person with
a guilty conscience.

For the third time I stood outside Mr. Morning's door in
the dim hallway. A noise was coming from the apartment;
it was as if a wind were gusting through it, a rush of sound.
I put my ear to the door and then I understood what it
was—the tapes, one breathy voice on top of another. He
was playing the descriptions. No one voice could be dis-
tinguished from another, but I felt sure that mine was
among them; I backed away from the door. At that moment
I considered running, leaving the box and tape recorder
outside the door. Instead I knocked. It may have been that
by then I had to know about Mr. Morning, I had to know
what he was hiding. I listened to the sound of the machines
being turned off and rewound one by one and then to the
sound of drawers being opened and shut.

When he came to the door, he was disheveled. His hair,
moist with sweat, stuck up from his head and two buttons
on his shirt were unbuttoned. I avoided looking into his
flushed face and turned instead to the now familiar room.
The blinds were still tightly shut. How can he stand the
darkness? I thought. He leaned toward me and smiled.

"Excuse my appearance, Miss Davidsen. I was sleeping
and forgot the time altogether. You see me in my Oblo-
movian persona—only half awake. You'll have to imagine
the brocade dressing gown, I'm afraid. And there's no Zak-
har, to my infinite regret."

When he said the word "sleeping," I felt a slight contraction in my chest. He's lying, I thought. He wasn't sleeping. He was listening to the tapes.

He went on: "Let me have the description and I'll shoo
you into the other room right away and then we can
talk. I've looked forward to your coming. You brighten
the day."

In the kitchen I looked for the box, but it wasn't there.
He's moved it, I thought, so I can't see what's in it. The
low sound of my voice came from the other room as I
waited. How many people had he hired to read those
descriptions onto tapes? What were they really for? For an
instant I imagined him lying in the unmade bed listening
to that chaos of whispers, but I pushed the image away.
Then he was at the door, motioning for me to follow him
into the other room.

"You did a good job with a difficult object," he said.

"Where did you get it?' I said. "It doesn't seem like a
very revealing thing to me, a bit of discarded fluff."

"That is precisely the kind of thing that is the most
telling and pathetic. It was there in your description—the
pathos."

"Where did you get it?" I repeated.

"She left it here," he said.

"Who was she? What was she to you?"

"You can't resist, can you? You're dying of curiosity. I
suppose it's to be expected from a smart girl like you. I
honestly don't know who or what she was to me. If I did,
I wouldn't be working on this problem. But that won't
satisfy you, will it?"

I heard myself sigh and turned away from him. "I feel
that there's something wrong with what you've told me,

that there's something hidden behind what you say. It makes me uneasy."

"I will tell you what you want to hear, what you already think you know—that she was murdered. She was killed in the basement laundry room of this building. She lived here."

"And her name was Maxine Robinson."

"No," he said. "I made that up."

"Why?" I said. "Why do that?"

"Because, my friend, I wasn't giving you the facts at the time. I was just giving you a story—one story among a host of possible stories—a little yarn to amuse you and keep you coming back." He looked at his hands. "And keep me alive. A thousand and one tales."

"It would relieve me enormously if you could keep books out of this for once."

"I can try, but they keep popping up like a tic, one after another, rumbling about in my brain, all those people, all that talk. It's a madhouse in there." He pointed to his head and grinned.

"What was her real name?"

"It doesn't matter. I mean that. It doesn't matter for what you're doing. A name can evoke everything and nothing, but it's always a boulder that won't let you pass. I know. I'm a specialist. I want to keep you pure and her nameless." He stared at me. "I'm not fooling you. I need you. I need your help and if you know too much, I'll lose you. You won't be able to do the descriptions anymore."

The emotion in his voice affected me. It was as if he had revealed something intimate, unseemly. I could feel the heat in my face. When I spoke there was a tremor in my voice. "I don't understand you."

"I'm trying to understand a life and an act," he said. "I'm

trying to piece together the fragments of an incomprehensible being and to remember. Do you know that I can't even remember her face? Try as I may, it will not be conjured. I can tell you what she looked like; I can recite a description of her features, part by part, but I cannot evoke the whole face."

"Don't you have a photograph?"

"Photographs!" He spat out the word. "I'm talking about true recollection—seeing the face."

The cat rubbed against Mr. Morning's legs and I looked at it. The room was cooler. "Could you open the window?" I said.

He stood up and pulled at the blind, raising it halfway. It was darker outside; a gray cloud cover had replaced the stifling yellow haze. I looked at his profile in front of the window. He stood there in his loose shirt and pants, his hand in one pocket, and I found him elegant. It's in his shoulders, I thought, and the narrowness of his hips. He must have loved her or hated her.

"I should get going," I said.

"You will do another description for me, won't you?"

I nodded. He gave me another small box, three twenty-dollar bills, and asked me to return in two days. I pushed the money into my pocket without looking at it and stood up. A breeze came from the window. The weather was changing. At the door he extended his hand and I took it. He held it for a few seconds longer than he should have, and as I pulled it away, he pressed his thumb into my palm. It startled me, but I felt a familiar shudder of excitement.

o

It had grown cool with remarkable speed. The sky was darkly overcast, and I turned my face upward to feel the first drops of rain as I strode home. I ran into my apartment and opened the box, pulling up its lid and pushing aside tissue paper. The third object lay before me on the table. It was a mirror, unadorned, a simple rectangle, without even a frame. Without thinking, I picked it up and examined my face, removing a bit of sleep from the inside corner of my eye, studied my mouth, the line of my chin, and then moved the mirror away to see more. I still can't understand it, but as I looked I was overcome with nausea and faintness. I sat down, put my head between my knees, and took deep breaths. It's possible that the dizziness had nothing to do with the mirror. I had had very little to eat that day and the day before. I scrimped on food for cigarettes, trying to keep my expenses down, and it may have been simple hunger, and yet when I think of that mirror now, it disturbs me, as if there were something wrong with it, something sickening.

Still unstable on my feet, I went to my desk and began to make notes. I was writing to myself, typing out questions about Mr. Morning and the project, but I couldn't put anything together. His remarks about memory, whispering, resurrection, returned to me as scraps of some inscrutable idea, some bizarre plan. And then I thought of the noise of the tapes behind the door, his touch and his slender figure in front of the window. Those letters, I thought, those letters on the page. What did they mean? A name. Her name. I moved the letters around, trying to arrange them into a coherent order. I found *mob, boy, dim,* and then *body.* The word coursed through me—a tiny seizure in my nerves. But it was absurd; a man doodles on a paper and I decode his meaningless scribbles. Besides, there were letters that could not be incorporated. *I. M.* He had circled the *M.* The suspicion did not leave me, and I began to imagine that rather than hiding, Mr. Morning really wanted to talk, wanted to tell me something, that the letters, the hints were revelations, part of a circuitous confession. "If you know too much, I'll lose you." I took my umbrella and went out into the rain.

Within five minutes, I was standing in the entryway of Mr. Morning's building. I buzzed the super. After a considerable wait, a small, fat man came to the door. He yawned and then raised his eyebrows, an expression apparently intended to replace the question: What do you want?

"I'm looking for an apartment," I said. "Do you have anything vacant?" This was my first ploy, and to my surprise, the building had one empty apartment.

"Three seventy-five a month." He raised his brows again.

"I'd like to see it."

He took me to the third floor and opened the door of a small apartment identical to Mr. Morning's. I walked through the rooms as if I were inspecting them. The man leaned against the open door with a look of belligerent boredom.

"I was told there was a murder in this building," I said.

"That was three long years ago, honey. There hasn't been nothing in that way since."

I walked toward him. "What was her name?"

"Your umbrella's dripping on me, sweetheart."

I moved it away and repeated the question. "Was it Maxine, Maxine Robinson?"

"Hey, hey, hey." He lifted up his hands and backed away

from me. "What's going on here? The name was Zalewski, Sherri Zalewski. It's no secret. It was in all the papers."

Tears were in my eyes.

"What's the matter, kid?" he said.

"Please, tell me," I said. "Did they find the person who did it?"

"You got some kind of special interest here?"

"There can't be any harm in telling me the story," I said.

He did tell me then. I think he was sorry for me or embarrassed by my emotion. Sherri Zalewski was a nurse who had lived in the building. She was knifed to death on a February night while doing her laundry. No one had seen or heard anything. A woman who moved out shortly afterward had found her the next morning. "Real ugly," he said. "Real bad." The woman had vomited in the hallway. The police never found the killer. "They snooped around here for months," he said. "Nothing came of it. They were after the guy in 4F for a while, a real weirdo, Morning. Even took him down to the station. All the tenants were calling and bitching about him. They let him go. Didn't have a thing on him."

"Do you think he killed her?"

"Nah," he said, "he's not the type."

From there I went to Butler Library to check the papers, but there was little new in them. Sherri Zalewski had grown up in Greenpoint. Her mother was dead; her father was a mailman; she had one sister. A friend, quoted in the *Times*, called her "an angel of mercy." Mr. Morning was not mentioned. According to the articles, the police had no suspects. Sherri Zalewski vanished from print for months; her name appeared only once again in a story run by the *Times* on unsolved murders in New York City. I found a single photograph of her—a grainy block of newsprint that was probably taken from a high school graduation portrait. I stared at the picture, looking for a way in, but it was unusually blank: a girl, neither pretty nor homely, with small eyes and a full mouth.

I carefully attached the chain lock on my door and turned on every light in my apartment before I sat down at the typewriter. I decided to write and record a letter to Mr. Morning. I did describe the mirror briefly, but there was little to say. Its surface was unscratched; it had no discernible odor; it was at the same time a full and empty thing, dense with images in one place, vacant in another. Except for the steady sound of the rain outside, my building and street were uncommonly quiet that night, but the noises I did hear made me jump, and I understood that I was listening for someone, waiting, expecting the sound of an intruder. He was in my head. Fragments of our conversation came back to me: Fern Luce, what he had said about not remembering the girl's face, the smell of wool and lavender in his mother's trunk. I wrote, and as I wrote, I saw her body on the floor in the vacant apartment I had visited. I always see it there for some reason—bloodied and torn apart. I see the corpse as in a photograph, black and white, illuminated by a dim light bulb. Even now when it comes to me, I can't examine it closely. I push it away.

Evening became night. The room turned dusky and a chill made the blond hair on my arms stand up. I wrapped myself in a blanket and wrote one page after another and threw them away. When I finished I had just one page. The mirror lay beside me shining in the lamplight. At around one o'clock in the morning, I spoke the words I had written into the tape recorder but didn't listen to them. The wind blew over my bed, and I fell into a deep, empty sleep.

Mr. Morning's rooms were cool and wet that day. His windows were open for the first time and the wind blew in, ruffling a newspaper that lay on top of a pile. His unusually pale cheeks were rosy and he seemed to be breathing more easily. I am quite sure that he sensed my apprehension immediately, because he said so little to me and in his face there was sorrow and maybe regret. Before I secluded myself in the kitchen, I noticed that there was a tall stack of papers on his desk that looked like a manuscript.

I didn't close the door to the kitchen; I let it stand open slightly and put my eye to the crack. I watched him as he placed the tape recorder in front of him on the desk and turned it on. He leaned back in his chair, let his arms hang limply at his sides, and closed his eyes. After a brief interval of static from the machine, I heard my voice come from the other room. I listened to the short description of the mirror that I had dutifully whispered onto the tape. Then I heard my full voice and saw Mr. Morning look sharply in my direction. I quickly shut the door. As I listened to the high, childlike voice that must have been mine, I clenched my teeth so tightly that later my jaw was sore.

"I know who she was. Her name was Sherri Zalewski. I wondered for a while if you hadn't invented her, but now I know that she existed and that she lived and died in your building. A glove, a stained cotton ball, a mirror. Why these things? Where did you find them? You must have known that I would ask these questions. I suspect that you have invited them, that you knew I would find out about her and about you. You should have told me the story, Mr. Morning. You should have told me directly rather than hinting at it. I do believe that, for you, this project is somehow an attempt to undo what happened that night, that these things are part of some elaborate idea I can't make out." There was a pause on the tape, and I listened for a noise from him, but there was nothing. "The things, the tapes, all your talk. I don't know what to do with them, how to understand them, how to understand you. I do know that the dead do not come back to life." I heard a loud scraping noise. He must have moved his chair. But the tape was still on. I pressed myself against the door, as if the weight of my body could shut him out. "I know the police questioned you, that they suspected you. I am not saying that you killed her; I'm asking you to tell me the truth. That is all." It was over. He was walking to the door and I heard him turn the knob on the other side. I stepped back. He was breathing loudly and a wheezing sound seemed to come from deep in his chest. He stood in the open doorway and stared at me, his face flushed. He looked as if he were about to speak, but then he closed his mouth and gained control of his breathing.

He said, "What is there to say? You expect me to confess, don't you, to fall down before you and tell you that I murdered her. But that isn't going to happen. It can't happen."

"What are you saying?" My voice was choked.

"I have already explained everything to you." He looked

past me and pressed his lips together in a spasm of emotion. "There is nothing more to say. The story is yours, not mine."

"What do you mean?"

"I mean that you've invented the story yourself. It belongs to you, not to me. You've already chosen an ending, a way out. I suppose it's inevitable that you want satisfaction." He looked at me. " 'The evil wizard turned to stone.' 'The king and queen lived happily ever after.' 'He died in prison, a broken man.' Whatever. What you've forgotten is that some things are unspeakable. That's what you've left out. Words may cover it up for a while, but then it comes howling back. A storm. A plague. Only half remembered. The difference between you and me is that I know I've forgotten. You don't." He turned around and faced the other room.

I spoke to his back. "That's what you have to say to me? I ask you to tell me the truth and you tell me that?"

"Yes," he said.

"I don't understand you. I don't understand you at all. Tell me that you didn't kill her." My voice was shrill.

"No," he said.

Mr. Morning walked toward his desk, and I heard the blinds rattle. There was a gust of wind from outside, and the papers on the desk were whipped into the air—hundreds of white pages flapped noisily against the bookshelves and walls, blew over the chairs and stacks of newspapers, sliding across the wood floor. Mr. Morning scrambled to retrieve them.

"Listen, Iris," he said. "I know things have changed, but I don't want to lose you. I want you to stay with me and do some more work. I want you to talk with me the way you've done these last two weeks. You will stay, won't you?"

I said yes to him. I thought to myself that if I did one more description, I could press him again, that he would tell me the truth, but now I wonder if that was really the reason.

He opened the desk drawer and took out another small white box. He held it out to me with both hands. "For tomorrow. Tomorrow at two." He gave me the tape recorder, and then after explaining he was short of cash, he wrote out a check to Iris Davidsen.

"I can't accept it," I said.

"Please, I insist."

I took it, knowing I could never cash it. I walked to the door, picking my way among the fallen pages. He walked beside me.

At the door he took my hand in both of his. "There's one last thing. Before you go, I want you to leave me something of yours." His eyes were shining.

"No."

"Why not?"

I released my hand from his grip. "No."

"One small thing." He leaned closer to me, and in the opening of his shirt I saw the cleft of his collarbone. There was a vague scent of cologne.

I opened my bag and began to search it, roughly pushing aside books, envelopes, and keys until I found an old green eraser, blackened with lead smudges, and thrust it into his hand, saying that I had to leave for an appointment.

I imagine that he stood in the doorway and watched me

rush to the stairs and that he continued to stand there as I ran down one flight after another, because I never heard the door close.

I ran into the street and began to walk toward Broadway. When I reached the corner, I paused. It had stopped raining and the sky was breaking into vast, blank holes of blue. I watched the clouds move and then looked into the street. The sidewalk, buildings, and people had been given a fierce clarity in the new light; each thing was radically distinct, as though my eyesight had suddenly been sharpened. It was then I decided to get rid of the things. I opened my bag, took out the check, ripped it to pieces and threw it into a large trash bin. Then I threw away the tape recorder and the unopened box. I can still see the small black machine lying askew on the garbage heap and the smaller box as it tumbled farther into the bin. It upset a Styrofoam cup as it fell, and I turned away just as a stream of pale brown coffee dregs ran over its lid. My memory of those discarded objects, lying among the other waste, is vivid but silent, as if I had been standing in the noiseless city of a movie or a dream. I saw them for only an instant, and then I ran from those things as if they were about to rise up and pursue me.

I didn't think that would be the end of it. Mr. Morning had my telephone number, after all, and there was nothing to prevent him from finding me. I waited for months, but I never heard from him. When the telephone rang, it was always someone else.

TWO

George was Stephen's friend first, and I suppose that was part of the problem. I had known Stephen for eight months, and even though we were often together, our love affair was fitful and uneasy. Stephen was secretive. He enjoyed withholding information—the identity of a caller, the place of an appointment, the name of an old friend, even a book title. I should have known that he was lost to me from the very beginning, but his body was magic then, and it drove me on. One look at his neck, his hands, his mouth, brought on a shudder of sexual memory, a pleasure that became a torment, because Stephen rationed his body, too, holding it back for days, even weeks, and I lived in a state of constant longing. Yet it always happened that just when I couldn't stand it anymore and had decided to leave him, he would come to me transformed: passionate, confiding, irresistible. Our harmony was brief. Usually it was a matter of hours before Stephen would retreat again. Sometimes I could see the signs of withdrawal in his face. His eyes became unfocused, his jaw rigid, and he pressed his lips together. But the truth was that even when I had Stephen in my bed, I often had the impression that he wasn't fully there, wasn't solid, and that if I wanted to, I could pass my hand right through him. I can't account for this feeling, but I'm certain that it bears on what happened later and is somehow tied up with that damned photograph.

I first saw them together on a cold day in early April. I

had just left Butler Library and had stopped on the steps
to button my coat, when I saw Stephen standing several
yards away in deep conversation with another young man.
They didn't see me, and I watched them for a few seconds
before I approached. Stephen moved close to the young
man, put his hand on his shoulder and whispered to him.
The intimacy of this gesture sent a tiny shock through my
body. Yet another person he has kept hidden from me, I
thought. When he heard me say his name, Stephen turned
suddenly and smiled, but I thought I detected a slight blush
across his cheeks and forehead. The other young man
didn't smile, however. He gave me a look so penetrating,
so laden with significance that I had to suppress a laugh.
"Iris," Stephen said. "This is George," and at that moment
it began to rain. The three of us huddled under my umbrella
and walked to the Hungarian Pastry Shop on Amsterdam
Avenue. I remember that George's shoulder touched mine
and that Stephen put his hand into the pocket of my coat
and through the layers of cloth moved his fingers up and
down the hollow of my hipbone. I turned my face to
Stephen's neck and saw him glance at George. He seemed
to want to catch his friend's eye, but George was staring
straight ahead.

We sat at a table near the back of the pastry shop and
drank coffee. Stephen introduced George as an artist who
took photographs, not as a photographer. The difference
was apparently a crucial one, because he emphasized it.
Most of what we said has escaped me, but the conversation
was lively, and George, who had been dour, brightened.
When he spoke, I heard a slight accent that I couldn't
place, and his words came more slowly than most people's,
which gave his speech unusual weight. I was glib, even

witty, or at least that's how I imagined myself. It may have been because Stephen and George appeared to listen to me with such rapt attention I was deluded into thinking that what I was saying had captivated them. Not until later did it occur to me that something else was at work, that George's presence had an effect on me and on Stephen, and that without the coffee with George, Stephen might never have taken me home with him that afternoon, and we wouldn't have made love the way we did, urgently, fiercely, as soon as the door was closed behind us.

I asked Stephen about George that same day as we lay in bed listening to the rain on the fire escape outside his bedroom window. Was he an old friend? Where had they met? What were his photographs like? But Stephen was reticent. No, he hadn't known George very long. They had met downtown at a party. The photographs were ingenious. That was the word he used. There was much he left unsaid, but it was impossible for me to know whether he was silent out of habit or whether George was a person he had reason to hide.

George began to call me. He invited me for coffee, lunch, dinner, and I went. We had long talks, and soon he knew my story, or at least most of it. George inspired telling. He was so easy in his manner, so kind and understanding, it was hard not to confide in him. But there was something else, too, something more important. George had a way of talking to me as if he knew me better than I knew myself, and in George this presumption was a kind of wizardry that turned loose thoughts and memories I had never spoken of to anyone before. I told him about Stephen. Perhaps that was my first mistake, but I was lonely at the time, lonely with Stephen too, and tired of worrying every sentence, of feeling that I had said more than I should have.

Unlike Stephen, George appeared open and frank, but in fact, he gave very little away, and sometimes after our evenings together, I would ask myself what I really knew about him. He was the only child of an American diplomat and had grown up in Europe and Asia. His father was dead and his mother lived in Brussels, but he rarely mentioned her. George must have had money. His photographs couldn't have paid for his large apartment and expensive meals. He did tell me about old girlfriends—a Swedish architect with whom he had lived for two years, a beautiful mime who had thrown herself out a third story window in Paris and lived, as well as a host of other female characters who had passed in and out of his life. But while he was remarkably candid about these affairs, chronicling their highs and lows in great detail, he spoke of them as if they were the comic stuff of another person's biography, and I began to sense that these stories, no doubt true, were nevertheless a means of evasion. They were too smooth, too complete, and I found myself asking, Where are the holes?

One evening in George's apartment—a large, white, nearly empty loft on West Broadway—he showed me a series of photographs. He explained to me that the pictures had been organized into pairs—an impromptu shot taken in the streets coupled with a studio photo. All the photographs were black and white. The first picture, taken at night, was of a very young prostitute stepping into a large car. My eye was immediately drawn to her elevated leg, covered to the thigh in a white boot that was oddly radiant. The picture was matched with one that showed shining car parts laid out on a floor—a hood, a fender, a bucket seat, as well as wires, tubes, hoses, and other innards I couldn't name. I looked at another pair. Two women sat in an open doorway smoking. Behind them stood a small child in diapers, its mouth gaping in a howl. The companion photo showed a sink with a woman's hands in rubber gloves and water swirling down a black drain. All the photographs I looked at evoked in me a feeling of mild distress. There was nothing lurid about them, nothing gruesome, and yet the juxtaposition of images was suggestive of a world askew.

I paused for a long time over two photos. The first was a shot that had been taken through a window covered with a grate. Through the diamond-shaped bars, one glimpsed a tiny room with an unmade bed, an old stuffed chair, and a remarkably hairy rug, but what had obviously intrigued George was a poster hanging on the wall. The image of a young woman in a bathing suit was obscured by the grate—her face couldn't be seen at all, but her well-shaped torso was perfectly visible. This photograph was paired with one of a naked young man cut off at the shoulders, his back to the camera. Behind him was a window.

"You like these?" said George.

"Yes," I said. I stared at the man's small, muscular buttocks and narrow thighs. I was reminded of Stephen and for an instant felt sure it was him. The recognition shook me, but bodies are very much alike, and the longer I gazed at the picture, the more I felt it was someone else. "How were you able to take the first one?" I asked George.

"From a fire escape," he said.

"Do you know the person who lives there?"

"No."

I looked George in the face. "My God," I said. "You go

climbing up fire escapes in New York City, snooping in
the windows of strangers. You could be arrested, murdered . . ."

George leaned close to me. He was unshaven. I saw the
tiny whiskers on his chin. What would it be like to be a
man? I thought.

"You like it, don't you?"

"What?"

"The danger of it excites you."

His smile irritated me, and I pulled away from him. I
searched for a retort, but none came. That night as I lay
in bed, I thought of several things I could have said and
mourned the fact that my wit usually bloomed late, peaking
when it no longer mattered, during the solitary hours close
to midnight.

The photographs George had shown me lingered in my
mind, but they were accompanied by other, more forceful
images of George on the prowl, roaming the city with his
camera, sidling down alleys and hanging from fire escapes.
I saw him perched on roofs and hiding behind dumpsters,
stealing photographs in the darkness, his flash igniting the
startled faces of those caught in an act they wanted to keep
secret—a kiss or a fight or an illicit transaction—and then
I saw George run from the spot like a burglar. More than
anything, the pictures had altered my vision of George.
The graceful young man with long dark hair and beautiful
manners had spawned a double, and it was this second
man, the one I didn't know, who fascinated me.

That Saturday the sun shone brilliantly, and it was very
warm. George had invited Stephen and me for lunch at

his apartment, and as I stood in the subway car heading downtown, I had a strong feeling of expectation. After we ate, the three of us walked up to the roof and sat on lounge chairs in the sunshine. We looked out over the city's other landscape—glistening tar flats, mysterious wiring, rusted pipes, and odd little sheds. We were listless from the food and the sun and said little to one another. We each had a book. I read mine intermittently and stared up at the clouds with dull wonder. They moved very slowly in the blue. Stephen was engrossed in his reading. He had rolled up his white pants above his knees, and his naked calves were pink from the sun. George had put his book down and was staring out at the city. His camera lay on a stool beside him. We were only four stories above the street, and the traffic noise was barely muted. George stood up and walked over to the roof's edge. I watched him place his toes over the side and rock gently backward on his heels.

"Don't do that!" I shouted at him. "It terrifies me."

George jerked his head toward me and extended his arms for balance.

Stephen looked over at George and shook his head.

Then I heard it—a scream, a loud bestial whine that went through me like electricity. For an instant I thought George had fallen, but I saw him rush toward me and snatch up his camera. Stephen leapt from his chair and raced to where George had been standing. I followed him and looked down into the street where a small crowd had gathered around a young woman who was collapsed on the sidewalk. A stream of blood ran onto the cement near her head, and I watched her arm fly upward, as if someone were trying to wrench it from her. Her whole body convulsed. The skirt of her dress was twisted around her hips,

exposing her thighs and the white rim of her underpants.
I heard George swearing as he fumbled with his camera
and film, but I didn't look at him. The girl lost one of her
shoes in a spasm, and I saw a man in the crowd bend over
and pick it up, but once he had it in his hands, he hesitated,
evidently unsure of what he should with it. He looked to
either side of him and then in one swift movement knelt
and put it back on the ground. Another man left the scene
and sprinted toward a telephone booth at the corner. A
woman in a red shirt had taken off her jacket and was
trying to cushion the girl's head with it but couldn't place
it correctly, and she cried out when she saw the head jolt
backward and slam the cement again. Someone was crying.
I heard George's camera click several times and then he
swore again. Stephen stood motionless, his eyes on the
street. My pulse beat in my head, and I felt surprisingly
cold, but I continued to look down. A man was shouting
instructions, his words garbled by a passing truck. He
pushed his way through the crowd and took the young
woman's head in his hands. Then I saw her urinate. A large
stain darkened the material of her dress and the liquid
flowed onto the sidewalk. The man held her firmly, her
face toward me, and I stared into it. It was swollen, red,
and smeared with blood. Her eyes were open but blank.
Suddenly I understood that she was choking. Her face
vanished behind the man. He was bent over her and I
think had a hand in her mouth. There were sirens. My
knees buckled. As I caught myself, I imagined my body in
the air, falling to the street below. I backed away from the
edge.

Stephen and George continued to look. George's camera
hung around his neck. Their faces, really very different,

resembled each other at that moment, their lips parted, their eyes narrowed in concentration.

"I think she's going to be all right," said Stephen. "She's in the ambulance now."

"That man saved her," I said.

Stephen spoke quickly, excitedly. "It's hard to believe a body can move like that. I've never seen a grand mal seizure before. I thought she was going to come apart. Did you get any pictures?" he said to George.

"It's possible," George said. "But I don't think so. The shutter jammed. I can't understand it." He rubbed his face with his hand. "I'll never get another chance."

Stephen nodded. "That's too bad."

I sat down in one of the chairs. "Maybe it's for the best," I said.

"What?" said Stephen.

"That there aren't any pictures."

"Why?" said Stephen. He sounded annoyed.

"Well, because it would be terrible for her if she knew, and it seems so invasive, recording a person's suffering . . ."

"You really believe that there are subjects that shouldn't be photographed?" George said. He spoke evenly and softly.

"Maybe I do," I said, thinking aloud.

"You believe in censorship then," said Stephen.

I looked up at Stephen. His face was tight, combative. "Not censorship," I said slowly. "That's external. I mean control from the inside. After all, pictures can lie, too, can convey falseness rather than truth."

"Really, Iris," said Stephen. "What does that mean, truth?"

I turned to George, who was squinting at me. "I mean

very simply that photographing an epileptic fit entails some kind of responsibility." I was startled to feel tears come to my eyes and turned my face so they wouldn't see.

George knelt beside my chair. "You're very pale," he said. "Don't take it so hard."

I repeated his last word to myself. It meant nothing, like a word from a language I didn't understand. That happens to me sometimes: a word, often a simple, ordinary word, loses its meaning and becomes gibberish. I stared past George and Stephen and noticed the weather had changed. Dark clouds had blocked the sun. "Let's go in before it storms," I said.

The three of us sat in George's apartment and talked. Neither of them mentioned the seizure again, and I felt sure the omission was on my account. The windows were open, and we heard thunder and then the rain came in torrents. George closed them and went into the kitchen to make us tea. Stephen sat on the sofa with me, his arm over my shoulder. It was pleasant in the big room, and I grew warm from the tea. George joined me and Stephen on the sofa. I sat between them, and I forgot what I had witnessed from the roof. To forget is ordinary. Even people in mourning, distracted by some little happiness, forget the dead, and I didn't even know that poor woman.

The rain stopped. The sun came through the large windows and lit Stephen's face. George had red tulips in a crystal vase on his table, and they too were suddenly illumined. I felt an acute sense of joy. It was then that George leaned over to me and whispered in my ear. "I want to take your picture."

I laughed. "Why are we whispering, George?"

"We're conferring in private, my dear," he said, and grinned. "This is between you and me."

"Well, then, between you and me, why do you want to photograph me now?" I spoke in a loud whisper. "We've known each other awhile. Why now?"

"What are you two mumbling about?" said Stephen, who must have overheard the exchange.

"None of your business," said George, still smiling, and then to me he said, "Because it just hit me—your unusual beauty, your depth of character and intelligence."

Stephen leaned back in the sofa, his eyes on me.

George and I were playing. I adopted the voice of a comic actress. "If you believe for one moment that you can lure me into one of your schemes with base flattery, you're sadly mistaken."

"Try the earnest approach, George," said Stephen. "That's bound to work."

"Done," said George. "Iris, I want to take your picture. You've inspired me. My request may appear to be a whim, but in fact, I've been pining away for weeks and have only just this minute worked up the courage to ask you. When it comes to photography, I never joke. I am deadly serious." He stood up from the sofa, knelt at my feet, and took both my hands in his own.

I giggled and looked over at Stephen. "What do you think?" I said to him. "Do I dare put myself in his hands?"

Stephen shrugged. I could see he had tired of the game. He glanced at George, who had put my hands to his lips. I moved my gaze to George. He raised his chin and looked at me with open eyes. "Yes," I said. "Whenever you like."

That "Yes" put me at risk, and I knew it even as I said

it. But I didn't care. That's what is so curious about the whole story. As I uttered the word, I knew I was sealing a pact with George and it couldn't be undone lightly. And more than that, when I sat beside Stephen on the subway back uptown, I understood that I had somehow hurt him by agreeing to be photographed. He didn't mention it, but I could read it in his solicitousness and in his renewed hunger for me. I wasn't sorry either. When the train jolted out of the Seventy-second Street station, he put his hands on my face and kissed me hard. There was anger in the kiss, and for that brief time I relished my power. By morning the mysterious attractiveness I had possessed the night before had gone. Stephen was sullen and peevish. He clearly wanted me out of his apartment, and I obliged him, but I left feeling miserable. Walking home, I had a sensation of tremendous emptiness in my head, chest, and stomach. It was so pronounced I had the fleeting thought that I no longer inhabited myself the way I used to. The "I" which had always designated the whole of my inner life seemed to have shifted elsewhere, and for a minute I stopped walking, overcome by my own strangeness to myself.

George called to confirm our appointment. I was to come to his apartment Saturday at noon. I should dress simply. That was all. Late Saturday morning I woke from a dream about George. I remember only its end. He was wearing one of Stephen's shirts and was pointing at a window the size of a child's block. The dream was an unpleasant one, and I shook it off before I looked out my window into the air shaft, craning my neck to see the sky. It was blue. A good day, I thought. I chose a plain black dress with buttons up the front, reddened my mouth with lipstick, grabbed a sweater, and left for George's.

The spring weather put me in a buoyant mood, and while I waited for George to open his door, I realized that I was smiling. He pulled me inside the apartment without saying a word and hugged me. I noticed my heartbeat quicken. The familiar room was brilliant with light.

"It's beautiful here today," I said.

George took my face in his hands. He leaned backward and narrowed his eyes in mock scrutiny. "You'll do," he said. "It's all there."

"What's all there?"

"Everything I want."

"That's not an answer," I said, moving out of his grip.

"It's my answer," he said. He held his eyes on mine; his heavy lids and dark lashes were unmoving. I looked at his mouth and found it beautiful for the first time.

George looked down at my feet. "I think you should be barefoot. The dress is good, but your shoes and socks are funny."

"Are they?" I said, looking at my cotton anklets and sandals.

"They're childlike."

"It doesn't matter to me," I said and bent down to remove them.

"No," he said. "Let me."

I sat down on the floor with my legs outstretched in front of me. George sat too, taking my right foot in his lap. He undid the buckle slowly and slipped the shoe off my foot. He was smiling. I watched his fingers gently gather the material at the top of the sock and pull it down my ankle and over my heel. He folded the sock and laid it over the shoe. Then he proceeded to the next foot. There was no hurry in him. His movements were methodical,

precise. After he had pulled off my other shoe and sock,
he held my naked foot for a few seconds, his expression
now sober. I leaned back on my hands and closed my eyes.
The room's brilliance left its red markings on the inside
skin of my eyelids, glowing through my blindness. I could
hear George breathing, then his footsteps across the room
and back, but I didn't open my eyes until I heard the click
of his camera.

"We've started?" I said. "Just like that?"

"Just like that," he said.

"I'm not sure I know what to do."

"Yes, you do."

I didn't reply. Perhaps I did know, after all. The sunlight
from the window was warm on my back, and I could feel
my hair loose over my neck. There is a pleasure in being
looked at, and I seemed to discover it all over again as I
sat there on the floor listening to the camera's shutter. I
lost track of my thoughts. Images and words passed
through my head in the way they do before sleep. I changed
position almost unconsciously. It doesn't matter, I said to
myself. Maybe that thought was the break, the change I
willed in myself without knowing why. The pace quickened. I heard myself laugh. We found a rhythm. George
jumped from side to side. He squatted, stood, knelt, and
I moved with him. He laughed, and I danced, carefully at
first, aware of my arms and legs, my waist and hips, seeing
myself as in a mirror, but then I forgot myself and moved
faster and faster. I gyrated and spun like a lunatic for
George, who shouted encouragements and took what
seemed like hundreds of pictures, stopping only to put
more film in the camera. My feet pounded the floor. I made

noise, slapping my thighs, beating a chair with my hands, and hooting with an exuberance that made me dizzy. My heart raced. I don't know how long it went on, but I remember panting from the effort, feeling the sweat in my hair and under my arms, and finally bending over in exhaustion. I looked at George. He grinned. He was sitting on the floor with his camera in his lap. I knelt down and crawled toward him, looking at his lean arms and beautiful mouth. I lifted my right arm and extended my hand toward his face, but something in his expression stopped me. I have what I want, it seemed to say. Don't come any closer. I dropped my arm and sat back, still breathing hard.

George continued to look at me. Drops of sweat had formed above his mouth and at his temples. He looked weary but pleased with himself, like a person who has just eaten well, and as I studied his face, with its high forehead and brows that almost touched each other, I recoiled from him. The intense pleasure I had felt only seconds before was gone. I watched as he ran his tongue over his upper lip. It was an idle motion, but for some reason it struck me as horrible, and I closed my eyes. What has happened? I thought. I didn't say anything to George, but he must have sensed the change. I walked over to the window and looked into the street. A man with a package in his arms was hurrying down the block. My hands shook. I turned, saw my shoes and socks on the floor, and bent down to put them on.

George stood over me while I buckled my second shoe. "Are you okay?" he said.

"I'm tired," I lied. "That's all." When I looked at him, I noticed his eyes had lost their sharpness.

"I hope something will come of it," he said.

I looked at the door. "Of what?"

"The pictures, Iris. Are you still here?"

"Sorry," I said.

"Sometimes I work for hours and there's not a single good photograph. On the other hand, it happens that I catch a fabulous image with one shot. You never know."

"It's a matter of chance then," I said, picking up my sweater from the sofa.

"Chance is part of it."

"And the rest?" I moved toward the door.

"The rest," he said in his slow, deliberate way, "is design."

I reached for the doorknob, but George moved and blocked my exit. "I-ris." He hung on to each syllable of my name, turning it into a call.

"What is it?" I sang back at him.

He leaned against the door and let his eyes move down my body. "You're transparent," he said.

I winced. "What do you want, George?" I said.

"That's the question, isn't it?" he said. "Maybe you should ask yourself the same thing." He leaned close to me and kissed my cheek, but he didn't pull away. He held his mouth to my face for several seconds and then kissed my neck.

"Let's not kill it," he said.

I took him by the shoulders and pushed him against the door, not hard but firmly. I could see his surprise.

"Be careful," I said. "I bite."

He laughed loudly and stepped aside, opening the door for me, and as I walked down the hall, I heard his laughter. "Touché," he called after me, but I didn't look back.

○

Stephen and I were to meet for dinner at Moon Palace, a Chinese restaurant at 112th Street and Broadway. He was late as usual, and I tried to read while I waited, but the book, a bone-dry treatment of heroines in nineteenth-century English novels, didn't hold my attention. With my eyes on the page, I thought about the afternoon. Again I asked myself what had happened. Had it been an aborted seduction? I remembered his lips at my neck, his long hair in my face. "Don't kill it," he had said. In the past I had given myself up to ephemeral pleasures, falling into bed with near strangers, and had no regrets. But those encounters had been simple. With George, I was lost—like a person in another country who can't read the signs. And George had taken the advantage. By claiming that I, unlike he, was intelligible—an open book—he had made me vulnerable. What he saw or didn't see, what he knew or didn't know, was almost superfluous. George had an appetite for ambiguity, and I sensed that he had created a cloud of doubt in me for his own enjoyment. He was titillated by the idea that he could manipulate my desire. That is what I feared. What sickened me was that I was implicated in this obscure relation. I had sought it, and my motives were muddled. George may not have been clairvoyant, but he instinctively knew how to probe the unspoken within me, and I had felt it begin to stir the moment he looked over at me, his face flushed with satisfaction. I felt a hand on my neck and jumped. Wheeling around, I saw Stephen.

I caught my breath. "This is New York, Stephen. You don't sneak up behind people like that."

"Sorry," he said, and smiled. "How's the model?"

"Why?" I said. "Did you talk to George?"

"No." His eyes widened. "I was only asking you how it went."

"Fine," I said.

He sat down opposite me. "Fine? That's all you have to say?" He leaned back in his chair and put his knuckles to his chin, examining me with another smile. "What happened?"

"Nothing. He took pictures."

Stephen reached across the table, grabbed my wrist, and pulled me toward him. I felt a surge of desire that irritated me. No, I thought, no. I tried to twist out of his grip, but he held me firmly and muttered under his breath. "You went to bed with George, didn't you?"

"Stephen!" He released me.

The man at the next table gave me a thin smile.

"It doesn't matter," he said. "You're free to do as you please."

I watched Stephen order the food. After the waiter left, he addressed me in a brisk voice. "You know George likes pictures better than people."

As he spoke, I felt my throat tighten. "What do you mean?"

"Exactly what I said." He stopped and pretended to look at something across the room. "He wanted to photograph me, too, but I said no."

The picture of the young man's body in the window returned to me. It wasn't Stephen, I thought. Of course not. "Why didn't you tell me?"

"Should I have?" he said. "You made your decision. I

made mine. They're completely independent of one another."

"Bastard," I said.

He lifted his hands in a gesture of false surprise. "I don't know what you're talking about."

We stared at each other. Stephen's eyes were clouded, disingenuous. Had he been negligent in not telling me he had refused to be photographed by George? It wasn't clear. Our intimacy had no rules. There was no contract between us. I felt the frustration like a clamp in my chest and jaw. Before I knew it, I had spoken like a fool. "You've never loved me," I said.

Stephen's face lost its tension, and I remember thinking how easy it is to speak in clichés, to steal a line from pulp fiction and let it fall. We can only hover around the inexpressible with our words anyway, and there is comfort in saying what we have heard before. Stephen had a ready answer. "I've always loved you," he said. "I just don't love you in the way you want."

Two days later, George called. "There's only one photo I'm really happy with, but it's extraordinary. I thought you and Stephen might come to dinner tomorrow, and I'll show it to you. There are several others that are very pretty, but they're not for me. They're not . . ." He hesitated.

"Not art," I said.

George laughed. "No," he said. "They're not art."

We were silent.

"I feel bad about that day," I said.

"You shouldn't," he said.

"But I do."

"Don't worry about it."

"You didn't mention it to Stephen, did you?"

"What would I have said, Iris?"

"I don't know."

"Is there something you want to say to me?" he asked.

The question stumped me. I didn't answer for several seconds. "If there was," I said finally, "I can't think of it now."

George laughed again. "Well, if you do, I'm always here. Are we on for tomorrow then? Eight o'clock at my apartment?"

"That's fine," I said.

"I'm looking forward to seeing you, Iris." His voice was warm with affection, and I wondered what it meant.

"Goodbye, George."

"Goodbye until tomorrow," he said.

I listened to him hang up the phone.

Stephen and I didn't go to George's together. I invited him, but he told me he was meeting someone downtown before the dinner. He didn't name the person and I suppressed my desire to ask, but that afternoon, as I sat in the library beginning a paper I had pompously entitled "Fictions Within Fiction: The Fate of George Eliot's Dorothea Brooke," I imagined Stephen's companion was a beautiful woman. Her form and coloring changed with my moving thoughts, but the idea that she existed remained to nag at me, and even though she was only a spook of my jealousy, I couldn't stop the surge of fantasies about her and Stephen. By the time I left the library, I had invented several elaborate plots involving the two of them but hadn't written a single word about Dorothea. At home

I changed my clothes three times, and arrived at George's twenty minutes late.

George opened the door, and I saw Stephen standing behind him. They greeted me in unison. Stephen's face was flushed and the sleeves of his white shirt were unbuttoned and pushed up above his elbows. Maybe the room is warm, I thought, but when I stepped inside, the air was cool and I noticed that the windows were open. I could feel George's eyes on me while I looked at Stephen, and I resisted the urge to turn toward him. George brought me a glass of wine, and I stood and listened to the night sounds at the window. I heard someone shout the name Paul. I waited for an answer. None came.

"You're quiet," said Stephen from behind me.

I spun around to answer him. His face had regained its usual pallor. He looked past me, and the aimlessness of his gaze irked me. "How was your date?" I said.

He gave me an uncomprehending look.

"You met someone this afternoon, didn't you?"

"Oh, that," he said. "It was okay."

"Anyone I know?" I listened to the whine in my voice with a detached fascination. It was a false question. No answer would have pacified me. I had simply given in to a perverse need to ask, to expose and torment myself, and as soon as I heard the words, I experienced both relief and humiliation.

"Oh Iris," he said. "Not another jealous fit."

I walked away from him. My desires had begun to sicken me. They had grown old and tyrannical, driving me like brutal masters, and I understood then that I wanted them to die.

While we ate, I spoke mostly to George, as did Stephen.

After dessert, George left the table and returned with a manila envelope, which he laid on the table in front of me. "Take a look at it," he said.

Stephen, who was sitting next to me, leaned close to watch.

I opened the clasp and pulled out the large photograph. Despite my anxieties about the afternoon I had spent with George, I wasn't prepared for what I saw. At first I didn't even recognize myself. The person in the picture seemed to bear no resemblance to me, and for an instant I thought George had made a mistake, had given me the wrong photo, but then I saw myself, and I had a peculiar sensation of recovery, of remembering a forgotten event, something unpleasant and disorienting. I tried to catch it, but it was like the fragment of a dream that surfaces for a moment during the day, brought forth by a sight or sound, and then retreats—as quickly as it came—into unconsciousness. I put the picture down on the table but picked it up again.

It wasn't a full-body shot. I was cut off below my breasts, and my extended arms were severed at the elbows. Photographs are cropped in all sorts of ways, and the results are seldom disturbing. The viewer fills in the missing pieces, but this picture was different. The convention didn't seem to work, and I had the awful impression that the parts of me that weren't in the photo were really absent. I didn't understand it at the time, but I've thought about it so often since, I've come to believe that this effect was created by the fact that what appeared of me inside the photograph was also fragmented. A long piece of hair was swept across my right cheek and part of my mouth, slicing my face in two. A dark shadow beneath my uplifted chin made my head appear to float away from my body. My whole face lacked clarity, in part because the light was obscure, but also because the expression I had was nonsensical, an inward leer or grimace that signified no definite emotion or even sensation. It was a face without reason, and I hated it. I am not that, I thought, and let the photograph fall from my hands to the table.

Stephen picked it up immediately and held it out in front of him. He made a sound between his teeth, a long breathy whistle I had never heard from him before, and his face, which I saw in profile, had collapsed into an unfamiliar softness. He gazed at the picture and nodded his head slowly up and down.

"Stephen," I said in a barely audible voice. He didn't acknowledge me. "Stephen!" I said again.

"What is it?" He didn't look at me.

"The picture, it's . . ."

"Astonishing," he said.

I tentatively put my fingers to his bare arm, but he moved it away from my touch. "No," I whispered to him. "It's terrible. You must see that. It's cruel."

He spoke in a loud, clear voice that shamed me. "What are you saying, Iris? Speak up." I looked around for George, who seemed to have left the room, but then I saw him standing on the other side of the room, leaning against the wall smoking. I caught his eye. He had been observing us closely. I was certain of that. But to what purpose?

"What do you think?" George said to me.

"It doesn't look like me," I said. "To be honest, I think there's something ugly about it—"

George interrupted me. "And what does Stephen think?"

Stephen lifted his head toward his friend. "I think," he

said, "that you probably don't know what you've done. It's all here, George, everything you were looking for." And with that, he returned to the photograph. His unblinking gaze reminded me of some animals whose eyes appear totally inert, almost blind, and suddenly I had the feeling that for Stephen I had become invisible. An unexpected turn had been taken, and I had dropped out of sight.

After that evening, Stephen was distant. Although he called me often, he seemed reluctant to take me to his apartment, and I was almost never there. We were at odds, and despite my firm resolutions to win him back with a weightless charm, the stone I carried in my chest made it impossible. With Stephen, I had become a sour, witless bore. With others, I could be light. Men I cared nothing about called me, and every once in a while, I accepted an invitation. On them my indifference worked like an aphrodisiac. Because I didn't want anything, I felt free and jabbered away, spinning out all kinds of silliness that seemed only to augment their desire. At the end of such an evening I would close my door on the hopeful face and go to bed alone, and as I lay there I would feel bad for the man I had left in the hallway and ashamed for the coquette in me—that ridiculous female figure who made her appearance only when I was truly lonely and sad.

The photograph surfaced in my mind from time to time as an object of regret, but I thought the worst was over and tried to put it behind me. Then after I had a chance encounter with him on the street, Stephen disappeared. I saw him with a little redhead, no more than eighteen years old. She was pretty, frail, and expensively dressed. They were talking, and in Stephen's posture I could see his intent. He was leaning over her, his shoulders hunched. I knew him. He didn't seduce with jokes. He carried women off on a cloud of seriousness. And then I ruined it for him. I approached them and embraced Stephen, asking for an introduction to the girl. Her name was Lily. "What a beautiful name," I said, watching Stephen's face harden. Before leaving them, I kissed Stephen's tight mouth firmly and passionately. As I turned, I saw her green eyes widen, probing him. It was over. I didn't look back. I ran home and threw four new glasses against the wall. Twelve dollars plus tax into the garbage.

Eight days passed. Stephen didn't call, and he was nowhere to be found. The carrel he used in the library was vacant. He didn't appear in the one class we had together and was missing from all his usual haunts. I fought my urge to telephone him and called George instead. He was the only one I told about the scene with the redhead, but I related the incident as a little comedy, and we both laughed about it. Although George had probably seen Stephen or had at least spoken to him, I knew that to press him for information about his friend would constitute a breach of loyalties, and I held my tongue.

On the ninth day, I couldn't stand it any longer. Armed with the pathetic pretext of returning a book, I decided to pay Stephen a visit. I walked the two blocks to his building, entered the outside door with an old man who knew me by sight, took the elevator to the fifth floor, and was soon standing outside Stephen's apartment. I took a deep breath and knocked. There was no answer. I knocked again more loudly. Still there was no response. He's out with the redhead, I thought. I knocked one last time and tried the doorknob. It turned and I pushed the door open. I stepped inside and called to Stephen without closing the door. From where I stood, I could see that the bedroom window was ajar. A draft blew across my face, and I jumped as I heard the door slam behind me. I tiptoed into the bedroom and, seeing no one, knocked on the bathroom door. Stephen's silence took on an ominous quality. He's dead, I thought. He's been dead for days, lying behind that door. I turned the knob and pushed, but it was stuck. Then I put my whole weight into the motion and nearly fell into the tiny bathroom. No Stephen. I looked back into the bedroom and noticed a half-drunk cup of coffee on the desk. When I bent over to see if it was cold, I saw the photograph, or rather part of it, protruding from under a magazine.

Seeing it there gave me a start. Stupidly, I had never imagined it out of George's possession. It was probably a copy. The very idea that there was more than one photograph jarred me, and I was struck by a fantasy of its proliferation—my image multiplied into the thousands, scattered like so much litter in the streets of New York. I pulled it out and examined it for a second time. It can't be as bad as I remember, I thought. I registered its parts: the face obscured by hair, the shadowed, empty neck, the arms cut at the elbows, the small breasts in my dark dress. What was it that had made me hate it? It isn't ugly, I thought. It isn't anything. Am I seeing it clearly? I studied it further and felt nothing. I recall noting the blankness of my response with surprise but continued to stare at it. I felt my head grow light as if I were going to faint, and I had a slight sensation of nausea. I grabbed Stephen's desk chair with my free hand and sat down, still holding the photograph. I took a deep breath and turned my attention once again to the picture. The image was changing. With more curiosity than alarm, I noticed a small black hole in the face. How can that be? I said to myself. It wasn't there before. But not for a moment did I doubt its reality. The hole grew, eating away the left eye and nose, and then the dread came, cold and absolute, a terror so profound it created a kind of paralysis. I was transfixed. The hole was devouring the entire image, the face and hair, the shoulders, breasts, and torso, and I saw only the arm stumps hanging there alone for an instant, and then they too were engulfed, but like a person in a dream, I couldn't cry out. There was no sound in me, and I watched as the hole began to swallow the picture's frame. I feared for my fingers but didn't think to drop the photograph. It was bonded to my hands, a part of my limbs, and then I was blind. I don't know when my vision returned. I must have lost consciousness briefly, but I remember that it was the light in the room I saw first, and it astonished me. Then I saw the objects on Stephen's desk. They came into focus slowly—blurry, nameless things from another world. I heard breathing and thought there was someone else in the room before I realized it was my own respiration, loud and uneven like an invalid's. The room returned to itself, and I saw the photograph lying facedown on the floor, an insignificant white rectangle.

It was over, and I could feel pain in my head. I suffer from migraine and am susceptible to nervous tricks and minor hallucinations, but I have never been able to write off these experiences as aberrations that are purely neurological, because while they are happening, I am convinced that I am seeing the truth, that the terrible fragility

and absence I feel is the world—stark and unclothed. That
nakedness is irretrievable. It is left behind in the raw,
voiceless place that exists beyond the muttering dreams of
everyday life, where you cannot ask to go but must be
taken. As I sat in Stephen's apartment, recovering from
what I had seen, I gave the vision meaning. It had been,
I told myself, a revelation of the photograph's inherent
darkness and a sign of an infection among us: Stephen,
George, and me. I wonder now whether it isn't dangerous
to assign significance to that which is essentially vacant,
but we can't seem to avoid it. We cover up the holes with
our speech, explaining away the emptiness until we forget
it is there. My head hurt, and I was enervated. I felt the
mysterious fog of depression begin to lower—a formless
burden I couldn't throw off. I heard a noise and lurched
forward in the chair.

"What the hell are you doing here, Iris?"

It was Stephen. I looked up at him. "The door was . . ."
I stammered over the word "open."

He glared at me. "I'd never rummage around in your
apartment," he said. "What do you think you're doing?"

"I didn't rummage," I said. "Where were you? I was
scared something had happened . . ."

"I was checking on Mrs. Stone. She's been sick, but that's
beside the point."

I didn't answer. Mrs. Stone was an eighty-year-old theo-
sophist whom Stephen had befriended. I had forgotten all
about her.

"What were you doing with it?" He walked toward me,
picked up the photograph from the floor and shook it at
me. "You've bent it," he said, looking down at it. "You
were going to take it, weren't you?"

I touched the painful spot in my temple and looked at Stephen. "Of course not," I said.

"Have you been talking to George?"

"What do you mean?"

Stephen looked straight at me. His handsome face appeared frozen and was very white, but his ears burned red. Those red ears had a calming effect on me, and I stared at them with interest.

He pressed the photograph to his chest like a child claiming possession of a toy. "What were you doing with it then?" he said.

"I was looking at it." My voice was so soft I wondered if he could hear me.

"What right do you have to look at it, to come barging into my apartment—"

"The photograph is horrible," I said.

Stephen held the picture out in front of him. His face regained its color, and his ears turned pale again. "I look at it all the time," he said. "Ever since I first saw her, I've wanted to know how she works, how it works. I've wanted to take it apart, break the code, but she's a mystery. George can't explain it either. You say it's a horrible photograph. I don't know what that means. You're making a moral judgment, but this face, this woman, is beyond all that."

"Stephen," I said. "It's a picture of me."

He shrugged his shoulders. "It's obvious you don't understand. Look at it," he said, holding the photograph in my face.

I turned my head. "No."

"You won't look at it?" He laughed in surprise.

"No," I said. "Put it down." I gazed at Stephen's bookshelves. I was so tired I wanted to lie down. Stephen made a little noise, a kind of snort, and I felt him grab my arm and pull me toward him.

"Iris, have you gone crazy? It's just a picture. Look at it!" He was waving the picture near my face.

I closed my eyes and jerked my arm away from him. "No!"

"You're serious," he said. "You're afraid of it."

I didn't answer him. Without thinking, I put my hand to my head. My scalp was sore. Stephen knelt at my feet and reached out to touch my face. He no longer held the photograph.

"What's going on, Iris?" he said, and brushed a piece of hair from my eye. "You're so pale. Is it one of your head-aches?"

His kindness made me weep. I must have sat there sniffling and honking into a Kleenex for a good five minutes before Stephen began to unbutton my shirt, his fingers at my throat, his mouth close to my ear.

In the morning I left before Stephen was awake. The headache was gone. I considered leaving a note but decided not to. On my way out I saw the photograph lying face-down on the desk. One look, I said to myself, one look to check, but I withdrew my hand. When I stepped out into the street, the daylight, the cool air startled me. Leaving those small, dark rooms is like coming out of a grave, I thought.

Stephen left town that day. He told me he was spending six days with his parents in San Francisco and was going to a cousin's wedding. I believed him. The photograph had become for me the experience of seeing it in Stephen's apartment. I couldn't separate the image from the hole, and although I could describe the picture with some accuracy, could name its parts, I was unable really to see it. Its presence in my mind was, in fact, an absence that I felt as a small but constant threat. That was quite bad enough, but what unnerved me altogether was that the picture began to turn up elsewhere, and I was gripped by the uncanny feeling that it had taken on a life of its own. I don't mean this literally. What I mean is that the photograph seemed to be in circulation—if not an actual print, certainly the news of its existence. The day after Stephen's departure, I was reading in the library and a young man I had never seen before sat down next to me and said, "You're the girl in the photograph, aren't you?" I was dumbfounded. He looked at me and laughed. "Jonathan Mann showed it to me." "I don't know anyone by that name," I said to him. "Really?" he answered. "Jonathan said he had met you." "I don't think so," I said, staring into the young man's face. Then he looked at the clock, sprang up from his chair, and ran to the door. "And who are you?" I called after him, drawing irritated looks from other readers. "Whorf," he said, "Ian Whorf—art history."

I used the telephone in the hall to call George, but he wasn't home. Who the hell is Jonathan Mann? George must know, I thought, and tried the number a second time. No luck. The next day it happened again. My linguistics professor, a big, friendly man with a white beard and a red face, stopped me after class and said, "I hear you have a second career as a model." He smiled at me. "Who told you that?" I said, hearing the strain in my voice. Professor Phibbs looked confused. "Over in the English Department office," he said. "Marge, the secretary, seemed to know all about it." "Marge." I repeated the name aloud. I knew Marge dimly. She was a small, officious woman who sat behind an enormous desk in the middle of the office. I tried to conjure an image of her talking about the photograph. Could Stephen have shown it to her? The whole idea was fantastic. I said goodbye to Professor Phibbs, walked to Philosophy Hall, and took the elevator to the sixth floor.

When I entered the office, I saw a young woman—she must have been a student—sitting alone in the outer room. She had a remarkable mass of brown hair that stood straight out from the sides of her head, and I looked at it while I spoke to her. "Is Marge in?" As I said this, I was stung by the absurdity of my errand. "No, she's out for a couple of days. Maybe I can help you." "No," I said. "It's a personal matter." "Would you like to leave your name?" "No, I wouldn't." My voice was too emphatic. "No thank you," I said in an attempt to change my tone. "Suit yourself," she said, and busied herself with a pile of papers on the desk.

I spent the whole evening calling George. I let the telephone ring and ring, but he was out. I also looked up Ian Whorf in the Manhattan book and found no listing. When dawn lit the air shaft outside my window, I was still awake, my bed cluttered with reading material—books, Xeroxed articles, magazines—which I had read through the insomniac hours. Finally I slept, a thin, restless sleep, full of chattering voices and anonymous crowds.

When I awoke three hours later, I went to the library and produced three pages on Dorothea Brooke, whose delusions had taken on renewed vigor, and then, exhausted, I walked to Philosophy Hall to have tea in the graduate lounge. This ritual, conducted entirely in whispers, took place every afternoon. A morose woman sat behind a large silver contraption doling out tea and small, pale cookies. We were expected to pay a quarter for this privilege, but the dish meant to receive the contribution was usually empty. Betsy Wingate was sitting in the far corner of the room, and she waved to me as I entered. I joined her after standing in line for my tea. Betsy was an acquaintance, not a friend. I knew her from a class on English Romantic poetry in which she had been strikingly articulate, delivering paragraph-long questions to Professor Kreeber, who had been known to sigh when she raised her hand.

"Iris," she said. "You're just the person I've been dying to see." She patted the chair next to her. I sat down. "Ralph was here a few minutes ago, and he mentioned you."

I must have looked blank.

"You know, Iris, the Derridian fellow with the ponytail. He sat behind you in the Romantics—you remember, the tall one."

I nodded. I remembered Ralph.

"He said that there's a stunning photograph of you floating around taken by a downtown artist. 'A study in eroticism,' he called it."

I caught my breath.

Betsy continued. "I have to ask you, as one feminist to another, you understand. Didn't you feel compromised posing in the nude?"

I looked into Betsy's enlarged eyes through the thick lenses of her glasses. The distortion made me think of dreams in which a single physical detail on a person overwhelms all the others. So I'm naked now, I thought. I gripped my teacup with both hands and stared into the

brown liquid. Everywhere I go, the stupid thing seems to
have been there before me. It's like I'm chasing it. Betsy
was waiting for my considered opinion. I was fully clothed,
I imagined myself saying. The photograph isn't what you
think, it's . . . Then I knew I couldn't explain myself.

"Not a bit," I said, and rose to leave.

She looked disappointed.

The room was warm, too warm. I have to get out, I
thought. I walked quickly to the door and through the
lobby, passing two people who were speaking in hushed
voices, and it occurred to me that they too were in on the
rumor, telling each other the news about the photograph.
They glanced in my direction. I paused on the steps outside
the building to collect myself. Butler Library rose up in the
sunshine, and I remembered Stephen touching George, his
mouth at his friend's ear. It had begun there, and now
strangers were talking. The course of gossip is invisible.
One thing becomes another, like the weather. Jonathan
Mann, Ian Whorf, Professor Phibbs, Marge, Ralph, Betsy
Wingate—the names blew through me. A day before, I
would have pursued it, tried to track the route the photograph had traveled, and confronted those who had
passed the word, but I understood now it was impossible.
I had no stamina for a wild-goose chase through the dark
halls of Columbia University listening to variant accounts
of my exhibitionism. I sat down on the steps, closed my
eyes and turned my face to the sun. Betsy's version was as
good as any. In the end nudity was a tame metaphor for
what had happened to me. I had not only been stripped.
I had been turned inside out.

For the next two days I hid in my apartment, writing
about Dorothea's desires and Casaubon's emptiness, stop-

ping periodically to call George, who was never home. It was then I began to suspect George and Stephen were in league. They had left the city together, after all. Perhaps there was no cousin, no wedding, and Stephen had lied to cover himself. But my suspicions weren't limited to the two of them. I had begun to feel uncertain in public places, to expect stares and questions, and as I walked into the library after my seclusion, I looked at no one. The morning and most of the afternoon passed without incident. With every hour that went by I grew more relaxed, and by four o'clock I was sitting very happily, picking through my copy of *Middlemarch*, when a strange man approached me.

He appeared from behind a trolley piled high with books that were to be returned to the stacks, a handsome man wearing a red sweater and sunglasses. He leaned over the table where I was working and looked down at me with a broad grin. His movements had a proprietary quality I disliked. He was too old to be a student, too flashy for a librarian. I felt sure no librarian in the history of the world had worn sunglasses indoors.

"You're Iris," he said, "aren't you?"

I looked at the dark plates over his eyes. "No," I said, "I'm not."

He looked surprised. "I was sure . . ."

"No, you're looking for someone else," I said. "Another person entirely." I heard the conviction in my voice.

He cocked his head to the side as if to see me better. "I could've sworn . . ."

"Sorry," I said, fixing my eyes on a paragraph. He loomed over me for a moment and then left. When I was sure he was gone, I looked up. My feeling of triumph was short-lived. In a matter of minutes the denial struck me as yet another turn for the worse. The ease with which I had sidestepped my identity alarmed me. I had done it before. A few months later, I would do it again, but that's another story.

I started for home, my book bag over my shoulder. When I came to West 109th Street, I passed it and continued walking. My mind was too full for that small apartment. A wind blew off the river, and my feet made time, became a pulse for my thoughts as I walked on and on. I had no destination, just the will to go, and I went fast, the noise of the city in my ears, its fumes in my nose and mouth. The books were heavy and my bag gnawed into my shoulder. I stopped at a delicatessen on Fifty-fourth Street and ate a large, expensive sandwich before continuing my walk downtown. The sky was deep blue when I finally arrived at Washington Square. I crossed it in the darkness, walking under the arch and onto the sidewalk. I shook my head when a man came close to me, his hand outstretched, his voice melodious. "Loose joints, loose joints," he chanted, and I thought of people wobbly at their knees and elbows like marionettes and walked more quickly.

The man vanished behind a tree. When I reached the other side of the park, I knew that I would walk to West Broadway and look for George, that I would sit on his steps if necessary and wait into the night.

When I put my finger to the bell, I didn't expect him to answer, but he did, and when I came upstairs, I found him alone, his apartment strewn with clothes and papers, an opened suitcase on the floor. I thought he would explain the chaos, but he didn't. "I have to talk to you," I told him, sitting down on the sofa, and I spoke without interruption for a long time, relating the peculiar events of the last few days, wondering aloud about the origin of the rumor, and as sanely as possible touching on the photograph itself and my extreme reaction to it as well as Stephen's. Throughout my monologue, I looked at George, seeking clues in his face, but though he was attentive, he displayed no emotion. I concluded by saying, "It's gotten out of hand. You can see that, can't you? It's gone wild."

George sighed. "It was probably Jon."

"Jonathan Mann?" I said.

"He's a dealer, Iris. There's going to be a show. It happened very fast. One of his artists is in the hospital and can't come up with the work, so he's asked me. I have the photographs. I want to use the one of you—among others."

"When did it happen?" I said.

"A week ago."

"You should have told me then."

"I've been gone."

I looked at a crushed blue shirt on top of the suitcase. "With Stephen?' I said.

He didn't answer me.

"Were you with Stephen?"

"For a couple of days. Then I went to Los Angeles."

"He lied to me," I said, "about the wedding."

"No, Iris. There was a wedding."

"I don't know who you are, George. I don't know who the hell you are."

"Don't you?" He looked sad. His dark eyes were bloodshot.

"When is the exhibition?"

"Next Friday."

"So soon? I didn't know it was possible."

"Apparently it is."

"I could ask you to take the picture out, you know."

"Would you do that?" He gazed straight at me.

I measured his face, but George looked only tired and very pale. He sat collapsed in a chair. All animation seemed to have flown from his body, leaving a still, wax figure. At the time I read this stasis as indifference, and it irritated me. "Maybe," I said. "Listen, George, I feel that I've been tricked, hoodwinked. I don't know where I am anymore, and that picture is part of it. I think you knew it would hurt me, but you went ahead . . ."

George shook his head.

"You robbed me." I didn't know what the words meant, but they seemed to identify an amorphous truth.

He looked at me squarely. "You came here. I photographed you. You came because you wanted to come."

I stopped breathing. He was right. I exhaled through my nose and listened to the small gust of air rush past my mouth. I breathed again. "Show it," I said, and stood up. I eased my book bag onto my sore shoulder. "But I won't be at the opening. I won't look at it. Stephen can cheer you on."

George held out his hands to me—his white face looked strangely swollen—but I ignored this gesture of reconciliation and went out the door.

I took a taxi home, watching my money tick away on the meter and remembering I owed Stephen thirty dollars I didn't have. I rolled down the window and let the air blow over me as the driver sped up Tenth Avenue hitting one green light after another. I read the neon letters that hung in the darkness over the street, suspended in the nothingness of hidden buildings and walls, signs advertising obscure products and places. I knew that some of them were names for things that no longer existed—dead companies, vacant hotels. This thought filled me with sadness, and I cried noiselessly in the back of the cab until it stopped at 109th Street. Before I put my key in the door, I looked up at the sky for stars. There were many that night, and their presence was as reassuring to me as the dreams of heaven I used to have as a child.

The next morning I was awakened by the buzzer. It was Stephen. I put on my bathrobe and waited for him with the door open. He came up the stairs, impeccably dressed in white, his hair shining in the sun that came through the hall window. He kissed my cheek, took my hand, and walked into the apartment. He sat down on an orange crate that was serving as a chair and put his elbows on his knees.

"George called me last night," he said. "You went to see him."

"Yes," I said.

Stephen bent his head. His chin touched the collar of his starched shirt.

"Too many secrets, Stephen," I said. "I can't live like that. They smother me."

"Everyone has secrets, Iris," he said.

"I know," I said, "but some are damaging and some can't be kept. They're bound to get out." I paused. "Like you and George. I feel duped. I feel that you two have been laughing at me all this time. I want to hear you say it, Stephen. Tell me now. Are you lovers?"

His green eyes fixed themselves on a pile of books I was

going to return to the library. Then he smiled and shook his head. "George isn't anyone's lover, not really. You know that. It's something else . . ."

I looked at his neck. The first two buttons of his shirt were opened, and I wanted to put my fingers on the small bones of his chest, but I held my hands back and folded them in my lap.

"He took your picture, though, didn't he?" I said. "That's you, your body in front of the window, isn't it?"

He didn't reply. He sat with his head down, and I saw him tremble.

"You lied to me about it, when we could have been open. We could have shared it. I felt so bad when I left George's that day, so abused and hurt, and you only made it worse. I can't understand it."

"There's no cruelty in you," he said, putting his fingers to my face and then in my hair. His hands smelled of scented soap.

"You're wrong about that," I said.

"You're good," he said. "I'm not. I'm a fraud."

"Don't say that."

Stephen smiled. "It's the truth."

"It's what you feel at the moment."

"It's what I always feel," he said.

"You always feel like a fraud. I don't believe it."

"I watch myself live, Iris, like a movie, and that image of myself is everything. I don't want to betray it. Do you know what I'm talking about? I'm telling you that what I can't bear is the ordinary. I don't want to bore myself, to sink into the pedestrian ways of other people—heart-to-heart talks, petty confessions, relationships of habit, not passion. I see those people all around me, and I detest them, so I have to be divorced from myself in order to keep from sliding into a life I find nauseating. It's a matter of appearances, but surfaces are underestimated. The veneer becomes the thing. I rarely distinguish the man in the movie from the spectator anymore."

I felt sorry for him and hated the feeling. He had delivered his explanation in a fierce tone of self-mockery and it bruised me. "I do understand you, Stephen, but don't you think that everybody is finally the same in the most essential ways? Some lives are probably much duller than others, but it's impossible to know how people live inside themselves, isn't it? I mean, a life could seem boring on the outside and be tumultuous within. Isn't cruelty more contemptible than ordinariness?"

Stephen looked out my window. He bit his lip and then spoke slowly without turning back to look at me. "I'm not talking about morality, Iris. I'm trying to be honest with you. I tell you sometimes it's cruelty that makes me feel more alive."

"Look at me, Stephen," I said. He turned his head. The pity I felt had changed me, and I smiled at him. "I don't want to disappoint you too much," I said. "But you aren't that mean. In fact, usually you're kind and filled with generous impulses."

He sighed. He looked so beautiful to me, so refined. He's right, I thought. He bears no trace of vulgarity, even though as the suburban boy of uneducated parents, he had been surrounded by it on all sides. He had made himself.

"And the photograph of me?" I said. "You knew about George's show that day you found me in your apartment, but you didn't tell me, and you didn't tell me either that you had shown the picture around Columbia . . ."

"I didn't show it to anyone."

"Someone did."

"Well, it wasn't me."

"And the show?"

"It's George's business."

I looked out the window at the brick wall. Its mortar was crumbling. "We'll never get past any of this, will we?"

"No," he said. "We won't."

My bathrobe had opened, revealing my legs, and I stared at my knee bones. "You're never going to come back, are you?" I said. My lungs seemed to close up.

"You don't have to be so dramatic," he said. "I'll see you. We can talk."

"No," I said.

"You won't even have coffee with your old friend?"

I shook my head.

"I'm sorry," he said. He closed the door very quietly behind him and never came back. I saw him, of course, from time to time—in the library, on the street—but because I went to great lengths to avoid him, our encounters were few. Stephen was out of my life, and yet I would carry around his ghost for months afterward—a beautiful, maddening creature that ate me alive.

Stephen left on a Sunday, and during the week that followed, I stuck close to home. I took walks in Riverside Park and continued writing my paper, which had become much too long. When I saw people I knew in the street, I hid from them, turning down another block or darting into a store, but that happened only a couple of times. My loneliness was an enforced indulgence. I left my phone off the hook. The photograph, the gossip, George's show, took on an unreal quality, as if none of it had ever happened. At night it would come back to me in strange, colorful dreams from which I would wake gasping, sweating, and largely forgetful. My seclusion was a form of burial I imagined would eventually make me well. It was imperative that I be seen as little as possible. I sequestered myself from the eyes of others because I had begun to feel those eyes as an almost physical threat. My skin felt raw, my bones ached, and I nursed my body with long baths and perfumed creams. My world shrank, became a cocoon. This isolation was a kind of punctuation, a way of announcing an ending to myself, and it wasn't without its pleasures.

Thursday night I was lying in bed with a notebook, outlining the final pages of "Fictions Within Fiction," when the phone rang. I had put the receiver back on the hook because it was after midnight and I expected no calls. It was George. I listened to his familiar voice and felt a tremor of expectation.

"I've been trying to reach you for hours. I'm at a pay phone down the street. I have to talk to you. I'm coming over."

"Please don't," I said. "I don't want to see you. I don't want to see anyone—"

"This is urgent. We must talk. I'll be there in a few minutes."

Before I could say another word, he hung up.

I washed my face, combed my hair, and waited. The buzzer rang, and I let George in. When he came through the door, he looked wild and spoke to me in a loud voice. "It's been stolen," he said.

"What are you talking about?" I said this calmly to make his tone appear inappropriate.

"The photograph," he said. "It's gone."

"The one of me?" I said. "Gone from where?"

"From the show. It was hung yesterday and now it's not there."

"You're joking," I said.

"Don't play games, Iris," he said. "You have it."

I looked at George. His hair was windblown, his beautiful jacket rumpled. My mouth fell open. "You actually believe that I sneaked into the gallery and stole that photograph? I said you could show it, and I meant it. What do you take me for, a madwoman?"

He smiled at me. "Either that or one hell of an actress."

"You mean you can't tell? I thought you could see right through me, George."

He took out a cigarette and lit it, blowing the smoke past my cheek. "Okay, let's say you didn't take it. Who did?"

"I haven't the faintest idea. Unlike you, I'm not able to read people's thoughts."

George sat down on the orange crate. I pulled the chair away from my table and sat down facing him. He said nothing but continued to smoke and study me.

A mental image of George's photographs in a large white gallery appeared before me. I remembered the poster girl seen through the diamond grate and the picture of Stephen that had been paired with it. There had to be two pictures. I felt slammed by sudden recognition.

"You're showing the series I saw, aren't you?" I said.

"Yes," he said.

"The pairs?"

He nodded.

"Then there's another picture," I said, "the one you matched with mine." She came back to me as I looked at George. She was writhing on the sidewalk, her legs and arms racked by the spasms, her red face and white eyes, her full, gagging mouth, and I turned my head away from him. I saw the city from the roof, and the clouds that had seemed to come from nowhere after it was all over. Stephen had said something about her body falling apart, and George had been mostly quiet, but he had taken pictures. I had heard the camera's shutter. I remembered the sound. Then I was crying. The tears ran down my cheeks, and I put my face in my hands. George reached out and touched my knee, but I pushed him away.

"How could you?" I stared at him and wiped my cheeks with my shirt sleeve. "What's it like," I said, "the picture of the seizure? I hope the urine stain came out well. You wouldn't want to miss that. I'll bet it's your masterpiece. Nothing like a heavy dose of human suffering to make a terrific photograph." I spat out the last word and saw the saliva fly from my mouth.

George didn't move.

"Did they take that picture, too?"

"No."

"Oh George." There was a wail in my voice. "Why didn't you tell me?"

He leaned forward and put his cigarette out in a cup on the table. "I meant to tell you," he said. "I was going to tell you tonight, but you didn't give me the chance. I wanted to explain it to you. Those pictures, those pairs, are studies in counterpoint. They aren't meant to be equations. The idea is that they play off each other. I intended them to be explorations—"

I didn't let him finish. "Garbage," I said. "Explorations of what? Your own brutal voyeurism?"

For a moment George looked stricken, but he recovered fast. "Listen, Iris. That was uncalled for. Do you really think that I should photograph only children with puppies or lovers in the park? Do you really believe that 'human suffering,' as you call it, is outside the domain of photography?"

"No," I said. "I don't believe that. What I believe is that your motives are less than noble, that you will happily risk friendships to get the right shot, that you're a kind of stage manager. You like to push people around, play with them, pretend you've made them. You did it to me the afternoon you took pictures. I think you already had the photograph of the seizure, and you wanted something parallel from me, and you got it. I don't underestimate your cleverness. I question your ethics."

"How eloquent." George folded his arms. "But I seem to remember a young woman who fell at my feet that same afternoon. You, Iris, you who have been moping about Stephen's unfaithfulness, were ready to jump. Are you prepared to argue that you're not responsible for your own actions?"

"No," I said, and fell silent. George was remarkably still, but I could see his chest move as he breathed. "I don't mean to sound self-righteous, but you've kept me in the dark about so many things, both you and Stephen."

George rubbed his fingers along the side of his face and said, "Maybe Stephen took it."

"Why would Stephen take it?" I said.

"He wanted me to withdraw it from the show. We fought about it."

"Because of me?" I said.

George turned toward the window. "That may have been part of it, but Stephen was a little crazy when it came to that picture. He kept saying to me, 'She shouldn't be displayed like that.'"

"Next to the other photograph?"

"No, in a gallery. He seemed to feel that it was sacred or something, that it would lose its power if I put it up."

"It's funny how he said 'she' when he talked about it. I never knew who he meant."

George turned back toward me quickly, his eyes small and his expression shrewd.

"Then again, maybe you took it," I said.

His eyes opened. "Now why would I do that?"

I leaned forward and rested my elbows on my knees, cradling my chin in my hands. "To keep it going," I said.

"To keep what going?" He spoke patiently, like a person tolerating a young child's irrational questions.

"The whole thing, George, the whole story of this stupid photograph. I wouldn't put it past you, generating a little intrigue for kicks."

"I'm flattered, Iris, really flattered, but I'm afraid you're wrong."

"Am I?" I said. "You need to stir things up, don't you? Your pictures are a record of that energy, that urge, but photography is a weird sort of intrusion. I mean, you're there and you're not there at the same time. You're the cameraman ghost, George, a man without a body, a man with subjects but no friends." I looked at George and wished I hadn't said it. He seemed old to me just then, his face haggard and his forehead wrinkled in an expression of pain. He was only twenty-six.

"You've summed me up very nicely," he said. "One short paragraph ought to take care of George. No need to give him a second thought. It's easy for you, isn't it? It's easy to write off the poor jerk who loved you from the first moment he saw you."

I held my breath.

"Don't look so shocked, Iris."

"What are you telling me?"

George was buttoning his jacket. He stood up. "I'm telling you there are many ways to live and many ways to love. I guess my way is more roundabout than most." He reached out and brushed my cheek very slowly with the back of his hand. "Goodbye, Iris."

I walked him to the door. He opened it, paused on the threshold, and then turned completely around to face me. "I have the negative, but I won't make a copy. A blank wall might be just as good, after all. What do you think?"

"I think you're probably right," I said.

George stepped backward into the hallway. He lingered there and nodded absently. Then he held his hands out in front of him, his palms toward the ceiling, and for a second I wondered if he wanted me to take them, but he let his hands fall and pushed them deep into the pockets of his pants. He swiveled on his heels and walked down the hall, cutting an elegant figure with his black jacket and long curls. I closed the door, locked it, and went back to my bed.

THREE

o

THREE

In the end they put me in the hospital. That was after all the other treatments had failed. The Inderal, the Cafergot, the Mellaril, the Elavil, the little white inhaling box, and the famous Fish cocktail. Every day I took the test and swallowed enormous blue pills of Thorazine at regular intervals. That was where I met Mrs. O. She was in bed three. I was in bed two, and Mrs. M was in bed four. Bed one was empty.

As a migraineur, I had low status. Admittedly, I was a bad case: I had had pain in my head for seven months almost without respite. Sometimes it was mild, sometimes brutal. My bowels were racked. I peed too much. I was supernaturally tired. I saw black holes and tiny rings of light; my jaw tingled; my hands and feet were ice cold; I was always nauseated. My body had become the meeting place for ridiculous symptoms, but what I had was still a headache, and headaches had little clout on the neurology ward. The day I arrived, the fat nurse said, "She's one of Dr. Fish's," and after that, they pretty much left me alone. They changed my bed and filled my water pitcher, but they rarely spoke to me. They seemed suspicious. And I didn't demand further attention, because I was guilty. It was clear to me that I had made the headache, created the monster myself, and just because I couldn't get rid of the damned thing didn't mean I wasn't to blame. Besides, speaking was difficult. I had to do it through a cocoon of Thorazine. The distance between the place where the words originated—somewhere deep within the headache—and where they had to go—out into the room—seemed impassable. In the beginning I was a quiet patient. It wasn't until later, after the incidents with Mrs. O., that one of the nurses called me a troublemaker.

Every morning, Dr. Fish would poke his head into the room and wave, and I would wave back and smile. But I knew he was disgusted. Dr. Fish was a man who liked successes. He liked them so much that before I landed in the hospital, he told me that I was improving when I was not, and now that I was so conspicuously unimproved, he shunned me. My person had become the sign of his failure, a recalcitrant body, a taunt to his medical prowess. Our relationship had been false from the start. I now believe that this dishonesty was rooted in Dr. Fish's method of interrogating his patients. He used a tape recorder. Had he actually recorded his patients' speech, this approach might have been harmless, but as it was, the only voice on those tapes was Dr. Fish's. When I arrived for my first appointment, he greeted me warmly, invited me to sit in a beautiful leather chair, asked me how I was feeling, and encouraged me to describe my symptoms. I told him that I had a painful head as usual, and was about to launch into the story of my headache when he grabbed a microphone from his desk and spoke loudly into it: "Iris Vegan. Case number 63912. Tuesday, September 2, 1980." Then he nodded toward me and smiled, a signal to continue. I had prepared notes about my headache on index cards, and looked down at them to orient myself.

"It started last August," I said. "I was walking home from the library on Broadway, and I remember that the street looked different to me, very clear and beautiful, and I felt incredibly happy. I even said to myself, 'I've never been happier than I am now.' "

"Yes," he said, and fingered his bald head.

I could see that Dr. Fish was restless, and although I wanted to explain that the feeling of completeness, of perfection, was essential to the story, I rushed on. "But as soon as I stepped inside my apartment, I felt a tug on my left arm, just as if someone had yanked it hard. I lost my balance and fell down. I was so dizzy and sick to my stomach that I didn't get up for a long time. While I was sitting there on the floor, I saw lights, hundreds of bright sparks that filled up half the room, and after they disappeared, I saw a big, ragged hole in the wall. That hole scared me to death, and the strange thing was that I didn't experience it as a problem with my vision. I really thought that a part of the wall was missing. I don't know how long it lasted, but after the hole was gone, the pain started."

Dr. Fish picked up the microphone. "The patient suffered a scintillating and a negative scotoma."

This ferocious editing had a peculiar effect on me. As the interview continued, I mumbled, coughed, forgot words, and lost track of what I was saying. Before I was sent to Dr. Fish, who was known in New York as the "Headache Czar," I had tried to tell my story to six less famous physicians, and each time, I had lost my tongue. I felt that if only I could articulate my illness in all its aspects, I might give a trained ear the clue that would make me well, but my words were always inadequate. And most of what I said was of no use to Dr. Fish either. He let it pass like so much irrelevance, interrupting me now and then for a curt synopsis. "The patient says that vomiting has on occasion relieved her pain."

Every week, I went to Dr. Fish, and every week, I looked better to him, less pale, less drawn, less tired. He interrupted me more frequently and summarized my complaints in an increasingly optimistic light. I couldn't see or feel these changes myself, but Dr. Fish was confident, and I half believed him. The truth is that I participated in the deception. I was studying for my oral exams then, and I was desperate for the treatments to work. If they didn't, I would fail. Of the 647 works on my list, 233 novels, plays, stories, and poems were still only titles to me. I had to know them by May fifteenth. Every day, I sat in the library, staring at a great work of literature that I couldn't read. My head was in the way, a stubborn, obfuscating cloud at best, an excruciating lump at worst. Measuring the degrees of my pain became an obsession. When my head lightened, I was jubilant. The pills are helping, I would think. But when it seemed to hurt more, I despaired. Mountains of books were piled on my desk, and as the days passed, the very sight of them threw me into a panic. Nevertheless, I pretended to be well. It was a point of pride. With Dr. Fish, I was always cheerful. I joked about my nerves. I smiled even when the headache raged and I had to hide my trembling hands by clasping them tightly together. Concealing illness from a physician is absurd, but I couldn't bear to be seen for what I was—a person going to pieces.

Then in January I was suddenly worse. I couldn't get out of bed. I threw up my pills and was leaden with exhaustion, but sleeping only seemed to aggravate the pain. After a week of unabated wretchedness, I dragged myself to Dr. Fish's office for my appointment and blubbered shamelessly in his leather chair. He told me to check into Mount Olympus Hospital the following morning.

o

I seldom left the room. All its particulars became familiar
to me: the tiny flaws and marks on the white wall adjacent
to my bed, the long, narrow cut in the Formica surface of
my night table, the frayed edge of my blue blanket. And
I spent hours looking at Mrs. O's bed curtain. One of its
rings was broken; this disturbed the symmetry of the fab-
ric's folds, and when the curtain was drawn, there was a
sag in the upper right corner. I can still see it perfectly.
My senses were oddly acute during that time. I wasn't
always able to open my eyes to the room's fluorescent glare,
but when I could, I saw its contents with remarkable clarity.
Every sound on the ward vibrated through me; my nerves
were as resonant as a tuning fork. The smell of antiseptic,
urine, and hospital food was often so pungent that I hid
my nose in the pillow. But at the same time, my body was
impossibly heavy; even lifting an arm required a huge effort. It was a curious state. I felt like a turtle hundreds of
years old, its soft inner body encased in a stone shell. It
was never clear to me if what I saw, heard, smelled, and
felt was distorted or if I was merely hypersensitive. At any
rate, things were not the same. I can't say what was behind
it—whether it was the drug, the headache, or my state of
mind. Probably it was all of these, but while I was there,
lying in that bed, the world changed. Mrs. O. had a lot to
do with it. She was the secret—the paralysis and the
frenzy—but I didn't understand that until the very end.

Mrs. M. was a woman who took charge. She had insti-
tuted a hierarchy in the room according to illness. In her
view, she suffered on a higher plane than either I or Mrs.
O. did. She had a nervous disorder that made walking

difficult, but her "mind" was unaffected, and she reminded us of this repeatedly. "Thank God, I haven't lost my marbles. That's the worst. As long as you've got your wits about you, you won't shame yourself." I ranked a distant second on Mrs. M.'s scale of maladies. She quickly surmised that my ailment, unlike hers, was psychosomatic, or as she bluntly put it, "There's nothing really wrong with you, is there? It's all in your head." Nevertheless, my neurasthenia rated far above the affliction of poor Mrs. O. Mrs. M. referred to her neighbor on the left simply as "the looney." Mrs. M. was supposed to practice walking but disliked it and walked only when the nurses insisted, and then she screamed at the disobedient limbs, "Move, damn you! Move, you idiots!" She much preferred sitting up in bed and talking. She went at it full tilt, babbling without pause, the bleached curls of her permanent trembling as she shook her head for emphasis. Her chief subject was money. "How do you expect me to get any service around here without something to grease the wheels, for Christ's sake? Green. I need green." Mrs. M. did get attention. I'm quite sure she bribed the nurses. They fussed over her far more than they did over Mrs. O. or me, and once, early in the morning, I witnessed a transaction. Mrs. M. dug under the corner of her mattress and pressed something into the fat nurse's hand. I suspect she paid them not to make her walk, because she did very little walking while I was there. She talked. She talked all day—to the doctors, to the nurses, to me, to her daughter on the phone, to no one, to anyone, about money, about Mrs. O., and every word clanked and rang in my sore head. "Look at the looney, will you? She eats like a dog. Yesterday lunch she ate Jell-O with her hands. She had gravy in her nose. Why did they put me in here? They should keep people like that separate, out of the way. I can't stand to look at it anymore. It'll cost me. It always costs me. I've got to get a different room—a private room maybe, with curtains, real curtains, not these cheap shades." When she wanted to count her money (this occurred at least once a day), Mrs. M. would remain seated on the bed but would pull the sheet over her entire body to hide the procedure, and I would hear her muttering the numbers to herself—"Twenty, forty, sixty, seventy, seventy-five, seventy-eight, seventy-eight dollars and sixty-two cents." When she spoke to her daughter, she always said that she had "no dough," but Mrs. M. seemed to have bills and coins hidden everywhere—in her bed, on her person—and whenever she moved, she rustled and jangled.

Mrs. M. meant to dominate, to fill up the room with herself, but despite her incessant chatter and her bulk (she was a fleshy woman with jowls and a substantial bosom), it was the small and silent Mrs. O. who took up space. She was a delicate woman in her late seventies, the victim of some nervous catastrophe. That event or series of events had left her incoherent. What remained was a fragmented being, a person shattered into a thousand pieces, but those bits of Mrs. O. inhabited the room like a crowd of invisible demons.

When I first saw her, she was lying motionless in bed, a frail, corpselike figure, but when I walked past her, she sat up with surprising energy and pointed at me. I looked at Mrs. O., with her extended arm and finger, her face alert as if she were waiting for me to respond. It was only when I turned my head away that she let her arm drop. I have no idea why she did it. It was an act typical of her only in the sense that it was unpredictable. One never knew what Mrs. O. would do next, and it was this quality that made life in the room precarious.

Given that Mrs. O. was a conundrum to everyone, she was the object of rumor, gossip, and speculation. Like most people confined to an institution, she had been divested of a past life. She was born old and in her hospital gown. I asked about her. I wanted to know who she had been and where she had lived. No one knew. Yet the ward buzzed with stories of her mischief. The very first afternoon of my stay I overheard two nurses talking outside the door. I'm certain one told the other that Mrs. O. had bitten a doctor. There was some mention of "bathroom nastiness" as well. Mrs. M. swore that Mrs. O. was violent and, moreover, that she was hatching a plot. "She's got something up her sleeve, mind you, and it isn't pretty." Later that same day, an orderly named Washington, one of the few people besides Mrs. M. with whom I ever had a real conversation, said that when Mrs. O. first arrived, she had spent one disastrous night roaming the corridors. He hadn't worked that shift, but a friend of his had caught up with Mrs. O. in the maternity ward at four in the morning. She was standing outside the nursery with her nose pressed to the glass. "Just looking at the babies, all quiet and thoughtful like." But later that day, various acts of sabotage were uncovered: the contents of a garbage can strewn in a stairwell, bed linens and towels ripped off the shelves in a hall closet and thrown to the floor, a missing food cart found in the shower stall of a bathroom. They were all blamed on Mrs. O. But how could she have wandered the halls without being seen? Washington couldn't understand it. Mrs. M. adamantly maintained that Mrs. O. was capable of disguising herself in a staff uniform and sneaking about the halls unnoticed. "The looney's crafty as hell," she said. But Washington had a different opinion. "How could that itsy bitsy old lady lift one of those giant trash cans?"

The next morning, a neurologist came to visit Mrs. O. He was a young doctor, vigorous and handsome. I noticed that his face and arms were deeply tanned. He strode over to her, sat down on the edge of her bed, and drew the curtain around the two of them. He greeted her in a friendy way, something on the order of, "And how are we doing today?" There was no response. I heard stirring in the sheets, a few muffled grunts, and then nothing. Seconds later, the doctor flung back the curtain and hurried out the door. He looked stricken. When I leaned over to look at Mrs. O., she was smiling broadly, and it was then that she reminded me of someone I knew or had known. I tried to dredge up the lost face and name, but they resisted me. This uncanny sense of familiarity subsided very quickly though it left a residue, a doubt that stayed with me. What had spawned that moment of recognition? Was it really something in her expression or was it something inside me? In any case, I began to watch Mrs. O. more closely.

The residents made daily rounds to give us the test. It was an unnecessary ritual, but I supposed they needed the practice. It consisted of a series of questions followed by some mild pinpricking. Frankly, Mrs. M. and I both enjoyed it. The test punctuated our day, and it was pleasant to be quizzed by those rosy young men in their white coats. Mrs. M. even primped for the occasion. She would pinch her cheeks and pat her curls when she saw a likely candidate coming through the door, and was visibly disappointed when the resident turned out to be female. Mrs.

O., on the other hand, was usually cantankerous. There
were a couple of days when she lay passively in her bed,
smiling meekly and nodding as the questions were posed
to her one by one, but more often she rebelled, and when
an examiner approached her, she would bat and kick at
him furiously, letting out one high-pitched shriek after
another. More awful, however, were the days when Mrs.
O. was eager to take the test. It always began with the
question "What is your name?" Mrs. O.'s face would contort
into a look of profound bewilderment. She would squint
and clench her jaw as she searched, desperate to extract
the correct words from her unyielding brain, and then her
small face would grow red from effort. It seemed that she
thought she could press out the name if only she pushed
hard enough. With each subsequent question, her straining
increased. "Where are you now? What season is it? What
is today's date? What is this object?" the doctor would say,
waving a pencil in her face. By the time he was pricking
her thigh with a needle and asking, "Can you feel this?"
Mrs. O. was exhausted and miserable. And despite the fact
that she couldn't reply to a single preliminary question,
she felt the pinpricks. One day she looked up at the resident
and said in a tired, plaintive voice, "Why on earth are you
doing that to me?"

The fact was that Mrs. O. wasn't one person, she was
many people, and no one knew who might turn up from
one moment to another. This plurality gave the room an
air of expectation, and I found myself charting the course
of Mrs. O.'s lunacy as if it were my calling. Every morning,
Mrs. O.'s husband arrived for his daily visit. The climate
of this morning encounter was often indicative of Mrs. O.'s
persona for that day, and I always tried to be awake for it.

He was tall and stooped, a man of clean, pressed suits and many ties. As Mrs. M. expressed it, he was "nicely pulled together." The person Mrs. O. had once been could be seen in him and in the things he brought her: a pale blue quilted robe with silk ribbons at the neck and waist, a small, immaculate toilet bag with pink flowers, and a shiny brass travel clock. When he arrived, he would walk slowly to her bed, place his offering of the day on the windowsill, sit down beside her, and take her hand in his. He did this without fail and regardless of her reception of him. One day, he would find a stone in the bed, a body so pale and rigid it might have been dead; on another, a flapping, writhing screwball who laughed so hard she choked on her own saliva. Or he might find her ruminating, her old face solemn with concentration. He took it all very well, witnessing his wife's metamorphoses with remarkable composure. I saw him excited only once. It happened in the early part of my stay. He had taken her hand, and I saw her turn toward him. Her face was completely transformed. The change was unmistakable. She knew him. He grabbed his wife's wrists and stared into her face. "Eleanor! Eleanor!" he called out to her, but she had already lapsed into forgetfulness. He hunched over in his chair, and I saw his back quiver.

When Dr. Fish said, "I'm going to put you in the hospital," I had felt immense relief. They'll take care of me, I thought. I'll get well at last. And when I'm out, I'll read and read. But I didn't rest in the hospital. Although my movements had been slowed by the drug, my brain raced, and I was breathing poorly, in little cramped gusts. Fragments of the books I was supposed to know came and went in my miserable head. I had memorized the first scene of *King Lear* and tried to recall it, but it had vanished. It was all nothing then, nothing and more nothing. I worried about the books I didn't know and the money I didn't have, money to pay for what my university insurance wouldn't cover: twenty percent of the bill. My headache would turn my parents into debtors, and there was nothing I could do. I was frozen in a hospital bed; it was impossible to know for how long. I had read once about an eighteenth-century English noblewoman who suffered from a headache for more than twenty years. I began to imagine that I would never get well, that I would die as a neurological footnote: "There is one reported case of a woman who was ill with migraine for fifty-two years. See Glower, 'Vascular Migraine Syndrome,' *JAMA* 1498, p.43." My parents called often. I lied, telling them I felt better. When friends called, I told them not to come. A few insisted, and they came with flowers and chocolates. During these visits, I always felt less pain, but after them, I was worse. I read the change as a further sign of my neurosis, and it depressed me. Stephen called. It was eight months since we had parted ways. A mutual friend had told him I was in the hospital. He said he was coming to see me, and I didn't tell him not to come. "Tuesday," he said. "I'll be there Tuesday at two o'clock."

During the day, I was able to restrain my growing alarm, but at night I entered a state of dread. This feeling was intensified by the fact that they tied Mrs. O. down at night. They did it after we had been given our medication, and after the overhead lights had been turned off. The procedure required three people, two to hold down the patient and one to secure the straps to the bed. The nurses called the device a "posy." When on, this canvas fetter resembled an elaborate and tortuous undergarment that took on a life of its own and sprouted appendages to foil the wearer. Getting Mrs. O. into this gruesome outfit was no small matter. She screamed, bit, clawed, and once as she fought, she said over and over, "What is it? What is this thing?" After they had left the room, she would begin the struggle to free herself. She shook the metal bars at the sides of her bed. She shook them, grunting rhythmically and without pause. She was indefatigable, an engine of determination. I don't know how long she kept it up, but it seemed to go on and on. It was the sound of the night for me, and I never slept until I was sure that she had given up. I watched and waited, because even in those first days before she had done anything to me, I was expectant.

I can't remember what day of the week it was, but on the morning of the first incident, Mrs. O., who had uttered perhaps twenty words since I first saw her, began to speak. It was a rambling, even idiotic monologue, but it had the tantalizing quality of an unfinished story.

"Where's my old Peter? I put him away, and now I can't find him. Oh, the songs I used to know, Lucy, every word by heart, every note as clear as day, and he used to tell me I sang like an angel. It was an open-and-shut case. They drowned him sure as if they'd held his head under water with their own hands, and not a single one of them went to jail. The last mean trick, I tell you. He wasn't right in the head, and they took advantage. I can't forget the two of them. They looked all pale and kind of stiff in their good clothes by the grave. Dirt poor, but decent as they come. And that dead boy was all they had." Mrs. O. clicked her tongue. "A sad, sad story." She shook her head. "Tell me the one about the lady on the hill, Eddie. You know, the one where she puts a cold hand on the back of his neck three nights in a row." I heard her humming a tune to herself, something simple and melodic.

About half an hour after the outburst, Mrs. O. turned to me and said loudly, "Don't just lie there, stupid! Do something!"

"Are you speaking to me?" I said.

"Of course I'm speaking to you. Who else would I be speaking to?"

Mrs. O.'s lucidity left me speechless. I looked at her face and saw something cruel in it, like the guilty smile of a child tormenting another.

I didn't answer her, and she seemed to forget me very soon. She wrung her sheet between her hands and bit at it distractedly. Within minutes, she was asleep on her back, her eyelids still partially open, and I could see the watery blue of one iris from my bed. I dozed too but was awakened by a sharp pain in my back. I turned and saw Mrs. O. standing over me. She was moving her thumb and index finger together like an angry crab. She reached out and pinched my cheek hard. I jolted backward and had an urge to slap her, but my arm was reluctant, too heavy to comply.

"Get up! Get up, sleepyhead!" she chanted at me, and grinned, displaying a row of small, discolored teeth. She bent over me again, waving those fingers in my face.

"Go away! Go away!" I heard my voice crack hysterically as I protected my face with my hands.

A nurse appeared. "Relax," she said to me. "She's not going to kill you. Up to your old tricks, are you, Ellie? Back to bed with you."

Mrs. O. smiled meekly, took the nurse's hand, and was led back to her corner of the room.

After that, I was reluctant to sleep. I have since asked myself why the pinching seemed so terrible. Her transgression had been minor, after all; the pinches hadn't really hurt. Perhaps it was that she had come too close, that my bed had lost its boundaries, and that once that invisible threshold had been crossed, I no longer felt safe. She would be back, I knew it. The chant "Get up, get up, sleepyhead" resounded like an annoying jingle in my brain. Why was she pestering me? She never interfered with Mrs. M. I was her victim. Why? Was it because I did in fact know her from somewhere, and she, in her own jumbled way, remembered me? It was impossible. I began to worry that I was not only nervous but mad, one step away from an asylum. Mrs. M. stopped talking about getting another room: Mrs. O.'s attentions to me were far too amusing. "She's got it in for you, kiddo," she told me. "Who knows what the crafty little bugger will do next."

Two days later, there was another incident. Again it happened while I slept. Sleep was irresistible to me then, and as hard as I tried to fight it, I couldn't keep myself awake all day. It began as a dream that took place in the bed where I slept. In the dream I woke and saw a body lying next to me, a warm, strangely wet body of a woman. I lifted her arm, but it fell lifelessly to the sheet. This person is dead, I thought. I've got to get her out of here. But then I felt arms around my throat and something heavy on my face. I need air, I thought, and an erotic sensation coursed through me. I opened my eyes. Mrs. O. was in bed with me. Her skinny arms were around me in a suffocating embrace. She was kissing me. I pushed her away hard.

Mrs. M.'s voice came from behind her curtain. "For Christ's sake, what's happened now?"

"She's in my bed." I bit my hand to keep back a sob.

Mrs. O. was crumpled up at the end of the bed. Her gown was untied and had fallen over a bony shoulder. She looked at me; her small wrinkled face was wet with tears. A doctor was at the door.

"What's going on here?" he said.

"She climbed into my bed while I was asleep. It's unbearable, just unbearable. Please, move her somewhere else. I can't stay here with her."

He looked at me and squinted, as if I were very far away. "We're making arrangements to have her moved, but we're too crowded right now. As soon as a bed opens up, we'll get her out of here. She's really quite harmless, you know." He smiled and pushed his hand over his balding head. "I'll make sure someone keeps an eye on her."

I didn't mention the kiss to anyone.

After the kiss, nothing happened for three days. It may have been that the staff was keeping a closer watch on Mrs. O. and she knew it, but I'm not sure. In all events, she was less active, more prone to phases of immobility and blankness. In the morning when her husband sat with her, I wondered what he would think if he knew that his wife had crawled into my bed and molested me. The kiss, always entangled in the dream, became a physical memory that shuddered through me without warning. The heavy, moist corpse and the withered old woman who had pressed herself upon me, her tongue in my mouth, left their fitful traces, and I was helpless against them. My pain had ballooned: it filled my whole head and seemed to enlarge my skull as it grew. I was all head then, a female Humpty-

Dumpty with four useless limbs. And I worried. I worried all day and most of the night. I worried about my head, about my exams, about Mrs. O., about Stephen's upcoming visit, and I worried about worrying. Anxiety fed my pain, but I didn't know how to stop it.

I looked terrible, and whenever I spoke, I panted and blew and embarrassed myself. Even Dr. Fish appeared concerned. He commented on my pallor and was clearly surprised that someone he had drugged so thoroughly was breathing like a steam engine. I was cold, too, and I couldn't get warm. One afternoon, a nurse brought me a pair of circulation socks. They were long affairs made of a white girdlelike material. They had no toes. I never knew the reason for this curious omission, but I wore them faithfully throughout my internment and still have them in a drawer, souvenirs of a time when my blood moved too slowly.

I fell into a world of only liminal consciousness. Always at sleep's border, I had to fight to remain awake. Mrs. M.'s patter took on a distant quality, as if she were speaking to me from another room. From time to time, I heard coins jingling. She's counting her money, I thought. But my ears had started playing tricks on me then, and it may have been nothing. Twice I heard my mother call my name. These auditory hallucinations were clear and loud. Her voice was there in the room, and the moment I heard it, I wanted to answer her, but instead I marveled at that inner voice and wondered if it wasn't another indication of encroaching madness. I was overcome too by loneliness, by a sense that I was shut inside a body that was going its own way. I've done it, I thought. I've created this huge, bad head, summoned the voice of my mother, dreamed up dead bodies, and generally caused my own disintegration, but how can I undo it all? I'm a ghost. Mrs. O.'s lady ghost—or perhaps she's mine, a revenant come to tell me something—my own half-naked little spirit braying in the wilderness.

The night before Stephen's visit, Mrs. O. broke out. My recollection of this event is confused, and I can't trust it. I know that they strapped Mrs. O. in as usual and that as soon as they left her, she began to writhe and shake just as she did every night. My pain had reached its zenith; it seared through the Thorazine and I lost all control of my breathing. I gulped and wheezed. I heard Mrs. O. rocking the bars behind her curtain, yet the noise seemed to be coming from within my own head. She groaned. I whimpered, but I wanted to howl in the dark like a wounded dog, to lose myself in an orgy of screaming. Instead I gagged myself on the sheet. Mrs. M. spoke to me, but I couldn't hear what she was saying—something about "the racket." I pressed my fingers against my temples. My nerves are erupting, I thought. Then I heard a loud noise, something being torn. I recall moving my fingers to my ears, as if that gesture could tell me where the noise had originated. The curtain across the room billowed, and then Mrs. O. was on the floor, her arms outstretched, her mouth wide open. It was much larger than seemed possible, a monstrous gaping hole in her face. I looked at her in the dim light of the room, her gown hanging like a rag from her shoulders, and I felt a violent jab in my chest, as if the wind had been kicked out of me. I tried to call out, but my voice was tiny, an inaudible squeak. I heard Mrs. M. bellow, "She's out! She's out!" Mrs. O. turned her back to me and headed for the door. I saw her flat, wrinkled buttocks as she ran stiff-kneed from the room.

The next morning Mrs. M. christened her "Houdini."
The name change signaled a shift in Mrs. M.'s opinion of
her as well. Contempt was now mingled with respect.
"Houdini's got spunk!" she said to me. "Tie her up, chain
her, send her to the bottom of the East River in a trunk,
and she'll find a way out. By God, she's got spunk!" "Spunk"
was the wrong word. Mrs. O. had will, a profound, unspeakable will. I don't understand what I saw that night
or why I felt knocked breathless. But the image of that
midget body as it stood in triumph on the floor and that
mouth, that terrible mouth, is now rooted in me and I
can't turn away from it. It's still frightening, and yet I find
it irresistible. I have a need to conjure it again and again,
to go on looking into it.

But that morning, the morning after it happened, I tried
to forget it. It was too recent, and I was a knot of misery.
My headache had eased some. It always did with daylight,
but my scalp was so tender that even the pressure of the
pillow was irritating, and my arms and legs hummed with
a peculiar energy, as if they were electrified. There's more,
I thought. There's going to be more. Mrs. O. had been
sedated, and she slept during her husband's visit and for
several hours afterward. I could see her through a gap in
her curtain—a shrunken body in the sheets. Mrs. M. slept
too. I waited for Stephen. At one-thirty I sat up in bed
very slowly, found my mirror in a drawer, and tried to do
something with my face. My hands shook. I was white,
and there were black pits under my eyes. Now I've lost
my looks, too, I thought. I managed to comb my hair,
rouge my cheeks, and put on a robe. Mrs. M., who had
just awakened, looked at me and said, "Must be a man."
Stephen was forty minutes late. He was always late. He

appeared at the door looking elegant, his long coat draped over an arm. He presented me with a small paper bag. In it were two books: a new translation of selected poems by Leopardi and a volume of poems called *Unearth* by an American poet I had never heard of. I thanked him. He was garrulous and distant. He must have been startled by my appearance but said nothing. I wished he had. I spoke to him without gasping and felt proud of my control, but my eyes were sensitive to the light and I had to squint at him during our conversation. The impression I made was apparently worse than I thought, because at one point he looked at me and said, "How did this happen?" There was incredulity in his voice. "Iris, you've got to pull yourself together."

I studied his face and impeccable white shirt. He's a foreigner, I thought. He has nothing to do with me. Perhaps I had loved him for that, for his bouts of astonishing coldness when he detected weakness in others. I disgust him, I thought. It was probably the first time during my entire stay in the hospital that I truly forgot Mrs. O., but as I looked at Stephen, I saw her behind him, still in bed but awake and erect. Her blue eyes shone and she leaned toward me. I didn't answer Stephen. Instead I looked at Mrs. O. I looked into her eyes and she met my gaze. She saw me. Stephen turned in his chair.

"Who is that?" he said.

"It's Mrs. O.," I said.

"What's she doing?"

"I don't know."

"Why are you looking at her like that?"

"Be quiet," I said. "She's going to speak."

He smiled then. I don't know why he did it, but I saw

his expression in the corner of my eye and remembered his sweetness all at once, but it was Mrs. O. who held me, not Stephen.

She had crawled forward to the edge of her bed and was holding the frame with her hands.

"What's the matter with her?" he said.

"Shut up," I said.

Mrs. M. answered. "She's out of her head, but she's got something for your girlfriend."

Stephen said nothing.

Mrs. O. opened her mouth. At first there was no sound, but then a noise came from deep in her throat and she began to call out, her eyes fixed on mine. "Eleanor!" she said. It was a short, urgent cry. "Eleanor!"

"By God, she's remembered her name!" said Mrs. M. "That tops it all. Bring on the interns! Let's have the test! The first question, please!"

"Don't," I said to Mrs. M., and surprisingly, she held her tongue.

Mrs. O. was calling to me. I knew it. We were both kneeling at that point and facing each other. "Why are you calling me?" I said.

"Eleanor! Eleanor!" she repeated. Her face looked desperate.

Stephen had his hand on my shoulder. He was pulling me back. "Iris, what are you doing?"

His distaste was palpable. Although he cultivated ideas that embraced the perverse and forbidden, Stephen was squeamish, and his adventures were strictly of the fashionable, literary sort. I saw him recoil. He gave me a look of disbelief.

"You can leave if you want to," I said.

"Eleanor!" cried Mrs. O. It was the same tone her husband had used when calling out to her.

Stephen had stood up. He touched my arm. "Do you want me to leave?" he said.

I did not look at him. "Yes." I said it very softly.

My eyes burned in the light. I saw Mrs. O.'s pinched little face. She's calling me, I thought. She's calling me. I leaned over the end of the bed and called back. "I'm here!" I called her as if she were far away, and as the sound of my voice came from me, it was as if a wind had blown through my body, opening my lungs and throat, and I called out again, "I'm here!"

Two nurses responded to the commotion. I heard Stephen say "Excuse me" as he went out the door. Mrs. M. was busy explaining, but I didn't listen. The truth was that I was indifferent to all of them. It didn't matter to me that I had made a scene. The exchange absorbed me totally. I called out again and kept my eyes on Mrs. O. Her small frame trembled as she stared at me. A nurse had her by the arm, but she managed to wriggle free. She was listening. I could see it. Her head was cocked and her face had a pensive look on it. Her thin white hair was sticking up in wild tufts. She hugged herself and rocked. She had stopped calling.

A nurse tugged at my elbow. "You're getting her all riled up," she said.

But Mrs. O. was still, very still. She lay on her back with her eyes open, but they didn't move, and her passive features seemed alien for the first time. She doesn't look like anyone I know at all, I thought. I lay back and closed my eyes.

The nurse scolded me. "It's been one thing after another

with you two. I really believe that you've egged her on.
You're a troublemaker, that's what you are. You should
have known better than to get her crazy. Imagine, toying
with a half-wit. You've gone too far!" I heard her march
out of the room. I didn't open my eyes. I began to breathe
very deeply and slowly, and I counted each breath. I
counted for a long time.

That afternoon Dr. Fish sent a psychiatrist to my bed. He
spoke to me kindly in a low voice, and he had a white
beard that I found reassuring. He didn't ask about Mrs. O.
until the very end. Instead he inquired about my studies,
my parents, and my friends. He wanted to know when my
headache started and what my other symptoms were. He
touched on the subject of my love life with great delicacy
and registered my response that it was nonexistent with
half a nod. I tried to speak in good sentences and to enun-
ciate clearly. My head hurt, but my breathing was much
improved, and I think I convinced him that I was sane.
When he finally asked me why I had been screaming at
Mrs. O., I told him very honestly that I didn't know, but
that at the time, it had seemed important to do so, and
that I hadn't been screaming but calling. He didn't seem
at all shocked by this answer, and before he left, he patted
my hand. I think I would have enjoyed my talk with him
had I not worried about what the conversation was going
to cost. He looked expensive to me, and I kept wondering
if his sympathy was covered by my insurance.
    A calm overtook my body that evening. The headache
sat firmly in my skull, but I felt less nauseated and the
vibrations in my limbs had vanished. I ate every bite of

my bad dinner and fell asleep very early. They had to wake me for my pill, and I never heard them tie down Mrs. O. I slept like a person in a coma and woke with difficulty the next morning. I remember that I had to push myself toward consciousness and that I had a sense of moving my arms in water and propelling myself to the surface. I was too drowsy to focus properly and at first I didn't notice that she was gone, but when I finally roused myself, I saw that Mrs. O. was not in her bed. The bed was freshly made, her belongings had disappeared, and the curtain was pulled neatly to one side.

"Where is she?" I asked Mrs. M.

"Beats me," she said. "She's not here. That's all I know, and the nurses aren't saying beans. I got the same line every time I asked—'It's none of your business.' " Mrs. M. lent her voice a nasal, officious tone. "And when I think of all I've done for those tight-assed cows and what I've had to put up with. No offense, but between you and Houdini, it's been a circus. I'll tell you what I think. Old Houdini had the last laugh. She did her disappearing act. Poof!" Mrs. M. snapped her fingers. "She vanished into thin air."

I looked at the empty bed. Since then I've often puzzled over Mrs. O.'s disappearance. Perhaps Mrs. M. lied to me. She may have seen them move the old lady while I slept. Mrs. O. could have had a stroke or seizure in the middle of the night. She could have died and been taken to the morgue. But I didn't consider these possibilities at the time. I was simply amazed by her absence. Had I not been so sure that my memories were real, I might have thought that she was my invention, a character I had blown to life for my own purposes. As I reflected, I felt a tiny spasm in my arm—the first sign of the crisis. It came fast, a brief but violent nerve storm, a quake in my system so powerful that even while it was happening, a part of me regarded it with awe. My arm moved again; it actually jumped on the sheet. I felt a surge of nausea and dizziness. I dragged myself from the bed and lurched past Mrs. M. to the bathroom. I vomited. My intestines cramped horribly, and then my bowels fell out of me. The paroxysm seemed to send all my internal organs into the toilet. I steadied myself on the sink and looked at my hideous face in the mirror. "You're a ridiculous person, Iris," I said, "a ridiculous person." I saw my head move in the glass. It felt smaller, lighter.

"Are you okay in there?" It was Mrs. M. "Should I get the nurse?"

"No," I said. "I'm all right."

I used my shoulder to push open the heavy bathroom door and then walked slowly across the room, clutching the back of my gown so that it wouldn't fly open. I sat down on the edge of the bed and remained sitting there for a long time. The light seemed unusually dim to me, and I looked out the window toward the stone-gray wall of another building. It was dark outside, and large snowflakes were falling steadily.

"It's snowing," I said.

"Of course it is," said Mrs. M. "It's been snowing for days."

FOUR

○

It all started with a handshake. I waited forty-five minutes to see him that day, standing outside his office with a crowd of other students who also wanted an interview. When it was finally my turn, I walked through the door and closed it behind me. "Professor Rose," I said. "My name is Iris Vegan." I reached across the desk and offered him my hand. He looked at me, and I saw nothing in his face. I might have been a stone. Then he lowered his eyelids. He didn't move. His forearms were hidden in his lap. My hand hung in midair, and I noticed that my fingers were trembling, but I didn't take it back. I won't, I thought. It can hang here forever. I stared at him and he continued to gaze at me. This went on for maybe half a minute. Then the corner of his mouth moved. It wasn't a smile but a tiny nervous quiver. He laid his hand in mine very limply. I squeezed it hard and sat down. I don't remember what he asked me or what I said, but I do recall his gray hair and green eyes, and that in this early memory he looks different from the way I would remember him later. The interview ended abruptly. "Thank you, Miss Vegan," he said. "I will expect you in class on Tuesday."

I had been admitted to the coveted seminar: Hegel, Marx, and the Nineteenth-Century Novel. Professor Rose couldn't have been much over fifty, but he had the mannerisms of an aging academic star, obviously beset by the affliction common to men in his place: contempt for students. At the same time, I found it hard to dismiss him, and I don't think it was only the rumors of his remarkable intelligence. Seeing him left an oddly sensual impression on me. It must have been his voice. He was wooden in his body, but when he spoke, the tone of his voice was highly changeable and sensitive, and it stayed with me—a sonorous trace in my ear.

The twelve of us—eight men and four women—seldom spoke in the seminar. Professor Rose would interrupt his monologue only to bark out a question. These inquiries were rarely open-ended. Usually they were factual, involving dates and names, but on occasion he would ask for an interpretation. That was worse, because we knew that the professor had a specific response in mind. Still, our intimidation made us unusually rigorous. And Professor Rose worked hard, intent on elucidating the miasma of Hegel. He read passages aloud and then took them apart, proceeding word by word, always referring to the German, and under the pressure of his examination there were moments of startling clarity. We read novels, too, and these books served as an escape from the tortuous road of philosophy. One afternoon in October, we were discussing *The Possessed*. It was raining outside, and the windows in Dodge Hall were clouded by water so dense it seemed to fall in sheets. Professor Rose was talking about the Russian Nihilists, his voice growing louder for emphasis and then dropping almost to a whisper. For a few seconds my mind strayed, and I gazed at the blurred red leaves of a tree in the distance and then examined the face of a young man with bad skin who was growing a beard. Maybe to hide his pimples, I thought. I heard my name and was torn from the reverie. "The bite, Miss Vegan," Professor Rose was saying. I turned toward him and looked at his face.

His mouth was still moving with the words "Stavrogin's bite," and I noticed his teeth when he spoke the character's name. "Yes," I said, straightening in my chair, trying to focus on the incident. "He bites Telyatnikov." My voice was small. "We know that," he said loudly. My face burned. "What does it mean?" "Nothing," I said. Professor Rose made a face and turned his head, looking for a more suitable reply, but I went on. "It comes from nowhere, out of the blue, and that's why it's so terrifying. It embodies nihilism for Dostoyevsky, because it's totally ungrounded and meaningless." I had been speaking at the top of my voice. He looked back at me, making his eyes small and sharp. The other students looked at me too. All at once I felt dizzy and clutched the table to prepare myself for the oncoming faint. It didn't happen often, but every once in a while, I would lose consciousness, just like that, for reasons I couldn't understand. But this time I didn't and recovered quickly. The professor continued speaking. I took notes and pretended to be absorbed in every word. When class ended, I hurried to leave, stuffing my books and papers into my bag. Then I saw Professor Rose standing beside me.

"Are you unwell, Miss Vegan?" he said. He put his right hand on the table.

"Oh no," I said, "I'm fine, thank you." I looked at him. He seemed to want to say something, but instead he stared out the window.

I pulled on my raincoat. The collar was stuck, and then I noticed that my book bag was caught underneath, making a bulge at my side. I yanked at the sleeve, painfully aware of my clumsiness.

Professor Rose smiled at me. "I'll leave you then," he said, "to your habiliments."

He took his umbrella and left the room.

I waited to leave until I heard his footsteps on the stairway. He had spoken to me kindly. I was certain of it, and with a rush of happiness, I understood that he liked me. This small encounter had a disproportionately large effect on me. I saw myself in relief, separate and distinct from the others in the class, and even though he didn't speak to me in that way for a long time, I began to regard Professor Rose as a secret ally. This transformation took place gradually, and I can't say whether it existed solely in my mind or whether he was responsible for it. I know that I started to look forward to seeing him on Tuesdays, that his face was pleasing, his severity undercut by humor, and that I read the assigned books with new zeal.

Ruth Slubovsky sat across from me in the seminar. She had a small face and long red hair. Ruth loved novels, and although she was abreast of all the latest literary theories, she had a gossipy interest in the fate of characters and liked to think of herself as a latter-day Emma Bovary. I never understood the appeal of imagining oneself as Madame Bovary, and I asked Ruth about this early in our friendship. In response she took from her notebook a reproduction of an eighteenth-century painting called "The Novel Reader." It showed a fleshy, naked woman reclining on a sofa with her eyes lowered and her legs slightly opened. In her right hand was a small, thick volume. "Does this answer your question?" she said, and laughed. I laughed too, but as became clear later, the joke was an aperture not only to

Ruth's dreams but to mine, and the image of the masturbatory reader, intended no doubt as a warning to the parents of young ladies, has resonance for me now. It was Ruth, after all, who introduced me to Paris, the strange young man who popped in and out of my life with the suddenness of a genie, and she became the unlikely yoke between what will always be for me two sides of a single obscenity: the image of the nude woman with her fat book and Paris leaning toward me with vigilant eyes and painted mouth.

On Halloween night Ruth took me to a party somewhere below Canal Street. I had been in New York City for only two months and didn't know my way around. Manhattan was a puzzle of isolated landmarks that I hadn't yet put together, but Ruth was a native and knew it by heart. She led, I followed. Because we had no money for costumes, Ruth borrowed clothes from her brother and we went as men. The suit she brought for me was right for my tall, thin body, and when I turned to the long mirror in my apartment, I was startled by the change in my appearance. It wasn't so much that I looked like a man but that the clothes created an image of sexual doubt. With no makeup and my hair hidden beneath a fedora, I seemed to be either a masculine woman or an effeminate man, and as I walked through the streets with Ruth, I lengthened my stride in imitation of a man's step and pushed my hands deep into the trouser pockets. Our journey ended outside a warehouse building. Ruth took me up five flights of stairs, through an open door and into a vast, crowded room. The light was dim and smoke blurred the faces of the guests who milled about with plastic wineglasses. From the first, I was struck by the almost lunatic pleasure the partygoers had taken in their costumes—both gruesome and ridiculous. Until then I had always thought of Halloween as a child's holiday, but gaping at the monsters, animals, transvestites, movie stars, and myriad others, I saw that the night of the dead looked more like an adult's fever dream—brilliant, chaotic, lascivious.

Only minutes later, Ruth spotted Paris.

"You see that little guy over there in the white suit?" she said. I looked in the direction of her nod and saw a tiny man of no identifiable age talking to a pretty young woman dressed as Alice in Wonderland.

"That's Paris," she said.

"Who's he supposed to be?"

"Nobody," she said. "He always looks like that."

"He's wearing makeup."

"As usual."

I stared at him.

"He's an art critic," Ruth continued, "known for his nastiness in print. They say a painter committed suicide after reading a review of his work by Paris in the *Village Voice*."

"He must have been unstable to begin with," I said. "Lots of people get bad reviews."

"I guess it was more complicated than that. You see, Paris knew him. They were friends, maybe more than friends, and Paris had always promoted his work. There was some girl, too, I think, involved with both of them. My brother told me that Paris knew this guy was on the edge. He took pills . . ."

"How awful. He sounds horrible."

"Actually," said Ruth, "he's charming in a way, and you

can't believe everything you hear. Maybe there's another side to the story. Anyway, Paris is everyone's uninvited guest, if you know what I mean. He's everywhere. Someone told me once that he hires a double to go to parties for him so he can be in two places at once. Look, he's coming over here," she said, leaning close to my ear.

The object of our conversation stood in front of me. I looked down at him thinking it would be difficult to find a double for such a person. He was too short and odd. I examined his small head, with its protruding ears and the cowlick at the top of his forehead that made his hair stand on end. I noticed then that the hairs had been forced into that position by a hair cream or gel. They were hard and shiny. He reminded me of an elf.

"Hello, Ruthie," he said, and then turned to me smiling. "My name's Paris," he said.

"Just Paris?" I said. "No last name?"

"No, that's it," he said. "It used to be something else, but I banished it."

"Just like that?"

He took a step toward me, lifted his chin, and lowered his voice. "Went to court, had the judge toss out the old and bring in the new. Legal magic. Since then I've been Paris, just Paris."

"What was your old name?"

"That's a secret," he said, eyeing Ruth for a moment. "My only real secret. I tell people everything, except that. Everybody needs one mystery, don't you think?" He looked at me, grinned, and then did a little cha-cha on the floor. Ruth and I exchanged glances.

Paris spoke to Ruth. "You don't mind if I steal her for

a little while, do you? I'll bring her back, or perhaps I should say bring *him* back. We wouldn't want to dispel any illusions, now would we?"

Without waiting for Ruth to reply, he folded his arm in mine and led me across the floor. I waved to my friend and looked down at my little escort. He seemed innocuous enough. We walked to a far corner of the room and stopped. Paris released my arm and said, "Tell me about yourself."

I gave him the brief, dull outline. I was the daughter of a linguistics professor and a Norwegian mother, born and bred in a small town, Webster, Minnesota. I had just come to New York for graduate school at Columbia University in literature.

He shook his head. "I didn't mean that at all."

"No?" I said, smiling at him.

"No. I meant something about yourself that would be revealing: an idiosyncrasy, a preference, a little story from your past. That sort of thing. It's a hobby with me. I collect what might be called psychological minutiae. Unlike most of this riffraff," he said, waving his arm to indicate the crowd, "who only enjoy talking about themselves. I'm genuinely interested in other people, in the state of their souls."

"I see," I said. "And you think that idiosyncrasies reveal people's souls?"

"I do," he said, drawing himself up to his full height of perhaps five feet. "For example, I'm asthmatic." He took a deep breath, as if to reassure himself that he was quite all right at the moment. "I love crime novels, all kinds, good and bad—it doesn't matter. I worship Giorgione, Pontormo, Egon Schiele, and Duchamp. And . . . " He raised a finger in the air and shook it. "I have a sensitive spot behind my knee, which I force my lovers to stroke. It drives me wild."

"I've glimpsed your innermost self," I said.

Paris smiled, then looked sober. "I like you," he said. "Now it's your turn."

"Okay. Let me see. I have no chronic illnesses that I know of. My literary passions are wide-ranging. I love Dickens and George Eliot, Henry James and Kafka. And as for my sensual inclinations, I usually keep them to myself."

Paris smiled without opening his mouth. He looked very white all of a sudden, like a mime. "I see," he said. "It's interesting though, isn't it, what's public and private? I mean, your taste in literature is there for everyone to see, but your taste in men is hidden territory."

"It makes sense to me."

"But all attractions are alike," he said. "They come from an emptiness inside." He hammered on his chest with his index finger. "Something's missing and you have to fill it. Books, paintings, people, they're all the same . . ."

"A lot of people do without books and paintings."

"True," he said, "but that doesn't affect the argument." Paris turned his head to one side and chewed on his lip. "Of course, nothing ever does the trick. Nobody's really satisfied for long."

I smiled. "I suppose not."

Paris lifted his chin and looked me straight in the eyes. His gaze was direct, ingenuous, like a small boy's, and I warmed to him. "Do you enjoy dressing as a man?" he said to me.

I looked down at the suit. "My costume," I said. "I know it's not much. Ruth and I whipped these up at the last minute."

"That wasn't the question," he said, holding his eyes on mine. "I asked you if you enjoyed dressing as a man."

"I guess so," I said, and hesitated.

His face was unchanged. "Does it give you a little kick?"

"Well," I said, not sure why I was answering. "These clothes make me feel different—especially on the street. I felt a certain excitement, yes."

"Maybe you feel like you've finally come home."

"I don't know what you mean."

"Don't you?"

"No." My voice was too loud.

Paris smiled.

The conversation had turned. I wanted to disguise my confusion but wasn't able to gain control of my face. I'm sure my discomfort was obvious.

"You're coming into focus now," he said. "I'm beginning to see you. I must have hit a nerve. That's what I was talking about before—little things, small revelations . . ."

He babbled on. I didn't really listen, but then he said more loudly, "I think I want to see your hair. Why don't you take off your hat."

I turned my head toward him. I had been looking for Ruth in the crowd but didn't see her. My cheeks were hot. "What?"

"It's a harmless request. Take off your hat."

I didn't answer. The room was so tightly packed with people that we were surrounded. I stood shoulder to shoulder with a woman in a platinum wig—Marilyn Monroe, I guessed—and on the other side of me was a tall man in an ogre mask. A cigarette in a holder stuck out of the opening for his mouth. A woman behind Paris was wearing a wide hoop skirt. He had to move forward, and his knee touched my leg.

"What's the matter?" he said. "I only want to see your hair."

"It's hot in here," I said.

Paris moved closer to me and put his hand on my arm. I stepped backward, bumping someone. "Watch it!" a woman said. I mumbled "Sorry," and felt Paris tighten his grip a little. He's too close, I thought, and took a noisy breath. I looked at his face and then at his fingers around my sleeve.

"You seem annoyed," he said. "Why?" His eyes were clear blue.

"I don't understand what you want."

Paris was inches away. "Iris," he said. "What's the big deal? I just asked to see your hair. If you don't want to show it to me, that's fine." He released my arm.

I reached for the hat and took it off. My hair, sweaty and tangled from the confinement, fell down over my shoulders and back. Avoiding his eyes, I looked away and swallowed hard. The gesture provoked some mysterious emotion and I felt my mouth tremble. "I have to get out of here," I said to him. I turned around and began to push my way through the crowd.

"You have beautiful hair, Iris," he called after me. "Where are you going?"

"I can't stay," I said, more to myself than to him.

I walked through the door, and once in the stairwell, I leaned against the wall, still holding the hat in my hand. What's wrong with me? I thought. I've been stupid. Why did I let him bother me? And what made me take off my hat?

I should have gone back into the party to tell Ruth I was leaving, but I didn't. I walked down the steps and into the deserted street, hugging myself in the cold night air. The suit was too thin. I looked around me and saw the subway entrance only two blocks away. I walked toward it fast. After a few seconds, I became aware of someone behind me and quickened my pace. Whoever it was matched my speed. I felt my throat tighten. Still, I continued to walk. The entrance was only yards away. I could hear the person breathing. A man, I thought. I broke into a run, using my whole body to propel me forward, and suddenly there was distance between us. I grabbed the railing to the steps underground, and before I sprang down them, I turned my head for an instant and saw someone disappear around the corner. He was small and wore a long black coat, but I glimpsed something white beneath it. Paris, I said to myself. And yet I wasn't sure. It was dark, and the man was gone before I could get a good look.

In the months that followed, the Halloween encounter with Paris assumed the quality of an apparition. The images I retained from that night were a garish jumble I couldn't sort out. I put the whole thing out of my mind. My costume was still in the closet, the hat resting on a shelf above the suit. Ruth had said she would return it to her brother but had delayed, insisting it wasn't urgent. He had lots of things to wear, she said, and I shouldn't worry. Every once in a while, I would finger the material of the suit, seized by an urge to wear it, but it wasn't mine, so I let it hang.

○

I had other business to think about, particularly my seminar with Professor Rose, which had become the focus of
my week. An unaccountable mania for knowledge had
overtaken me, and I read day and night, memorizing sig-
nificant passages, poring over criticism and history. I
crammed so much information into my head that when I
closed my eyes at night, I saw a printed page before me,
and isolated words and phrases from my reading churned
in my brain. Sometimes just before I dropped into sleep,
I heard little voices speaking to me in cryptic sentences or
monosyllabic outbursts. Despite my efforts, I was something less than a model student, subject to passionate erup-
tions in class and wild excursions into related topics. At
home I rehearsed calm deliveries, practiced lowering my
voice to make it sound authoritative and cool, but in the
heat of the moment, I would always forget. My voice qua-
vered, my heart pounded, my hands shook. I lost control
and the words came in torrents. I was serious, all right.
What I lacked was method and a scholarly temperament.
In early December I read my paper on Flaubert's *Senti-
mental Education* aloud to the class and was so moved by
my own words that I felt tears in my eyes during the last
paragraph. Yet Professor Rose and the other students were
kind. No one laughed. My teacher looked over at me from
his seat at the head of the table and said in a big voice, "A
little scattered perhaps, Miss Vegan, but a fine piece of
work." Then he returned to his notes. My happiness was
great, and when the professor stopped me after class and
proposed that I be his research assistant the following se-

mester, I embarrassed myself and gushed. "That would be wonderful," I said, and clasped my hands together under my chin. Then, embarrassed, I let them drop.

He smiled. I saw the wrinkles around his eyes deepen. "I'm a taskmaster," he said. "I work my assistants hard. Perhaps you'll regret it."

"Oh no," I said. "Never."

I began working for him in January, and at first there was nothing unusual about our meetings. He gave me German articles to read and summarize—abstruse, convoluted essays written in a language that baffled me. Every Thursday, he would hand me a sheaf of Xeroxed pages and my heart would sink. Then I would go home and look down at the incomprehensible sentences—clause after clause of dense, alien vocabulary, the verbs lagging far behind—and begin the tedious dissection. Meaning came in bolts. All at once I would discover the sense, identify the shifts in logic, and in the end I took pride in transforming the long, verbose essays into a single page of lucid words. But for the most part, these articles left me cold, and there were times when I couldn't resist commentary in parentheses, pointing out the flaws in the argument, unfounded leaps of faith, or the pointlessness of the entire thing. Professor Rose was amused by my arrogance and said to me once, "I think you can dispense with the editorializing, Miss Vegan. I am able to draw my own conclusions." He said this gently, however, and it made me think he didn't really mind.

In February our real work began. The German novella we translated together became the vehicle for a twist in our relations. Without it, I'm convinced, nothing would have happened. We would have remained as we were, professor and student, locked in the formality of the two roles. *The Brutal Boy* changed all that, blurring the lines of convention and muting our inhibitions. It took a long time for its effects to be played out fully, but I think they were profound. I don't mean to blame a work of fiction for my own behavior. That would be stretching the truth. I'm saying that the story was a door to another place, and in the end we chose to open it and cross the threshold.

One Thursday morning, I entered Professor Rose's office at the appointed hour and found him seated near the window staring outside. He didn't turn to greet me for several seconds. Instead he spoke to the window. "Do you know the name Johann Krüger, Miss Vegan?"

"No," I said. "I don't."

He swiveled around in his chair. "Well, you're not alone. He's been forgotten."

"Who is he?" I said.

"A German writer. He published a book of short stories and a novella. It's the novella I'm interested in—*Der Brutale Junge*, written in 1936, but it wasn't published until after his death."

He squinted at me.

"Yes?" I said.

"He died in a camp."

"He was Jewish?"

"No, homosexual."

I looked past Professor Rose and out the window, allowing his words to settle, trying to find a place for at least that single death among millions. I said nothing.

Professor Rose leaned forward in his chair. "He was thirty-two years old when he died."

I looked at him. He moved his hand toward mine. Then

he withdrew it, made a fist, and gently pounded a pile of papers.

"Anyway," he said. "We're going to translate this story together. You'll do it first and then we'll edit it together."

He handed me a small green hardcover book. I fingered the letters on its spine. I wanted to linger, to keep talking, but Professor Rose nodded at the door, and I hurried through it without saying goodbye. When I left the building, I noticed that it had started to snow.

I read the story that night in bed. It was written in a clear, simple German that made my dictionary almost unnecessary. The snow, illumined by my bedside lamp, continued to fall outside the window. "Klaus was a good boy," the story began. "He was ten years old, did well in school, was obedient, kind, and loyal." I didn't reflect on meanings then. The story was only itself, a thing apart, but I read without boredom.

Klaus's father is a successful surgeon, despite the handicap of a club foot. His mother, the narrator writes, is pretty, silly, and devoted to her son. When she speaks of him to her friends, she always says, "Klaus is a good boy, not a shred of nonsense in him." Poor Klaus, I thought, the nonsense is bound to come. And it does. The child begins to be troubled by cruel fantasies that appear in his head without warning. The descriptions of these sadistic daydreams are rendered with immense care, cataloged one after another in detail. Seeing a helpless old woman on the street, Klaus is overcome by a desire to trip her. While looking in his mother's sewing box, he thinks of piercing his dog's eyes with a needle. He loves the dog and can't imagine why the idea pops into his head. He devises ingenious ways to torment his best friend, Dieter, pulling

out his blond hairs one by one, wiggling his kneecap loose,
and hanging him upside down from a lamp in his room.
His fantasies become a preoccupation, a private indulgence,
a world in which ordinary objects become instruments of
torture: curtain rods, pillows, vases, cutlery. The delight
these notions bring him is offset by a terrible remorse
afterward, and he begins to try to ward them off. He prays,
recites the multiplication tables and poems he has memorized for school, but none of it does any good. Klaus
begins to fear himself, particularly in the evenings after
dark. He lies in bed with his hands underneath him, afraid
they will act without his permission. After several nights
of this, his agitation gets the better of him, and the boy
starts roaming. In the beginning he stays in the house,
padding through the rooms and corridors when everyone
sleeps, touching forbidden objects: his father's pipe, his
mother's porcelain figurines. His violation is meticulous.
He lets his fingers caress all parts of a thing before he
returns it to its place. But the enjoyment he gets from these
first misdemeanors dulls and, emboldened, he seeks new
pleasures. Klaus then commits small acts of domestic sabotage. With a pair of scissors, he cuts a nearly invisible
hole in his sheet. He hides several spoons. He ruins a
number of his own toys, hiding the decapitated soldiers,
wrecked train, and damaged sailboat in his closet. Then
one night, the boy leaves the house and once in Krüger's
city, designated only by the letter S., he celebrates his
freedom. He is happy just to walk where he should not
walk and see what he should not see, finding odd streets
and peering through the windows of closed shops and lit
saloons. The night is a chaos of sights and smells and
sounds, and the child becomes a tiny voyeur of the city's

secrets, a hidden witness to street brawls and soliciting prostitutes. Clad in white pajamas, he darts from one hiding place to another, venturing farther and farther from his own neighborhood. The boy's nocturnal escapades leave him exhausted and he falls asleep in school and cannot concentrate on his studies, but he is not discovered. On one of his forays he comes across a cat, a ragged, injured alley cat lying near a heap of garbage in a dead end just around the corner from a noisy bar. Klaus bends down to investigate. Reaching for the cat, he tries to stroke it, but the frightened animal scratches him, and the boy has a sudden urge to kill it. In a soft voice he says, "I'm going to hurt you," and then he strikes it. The creature howls but its damaged leg prevents it from escaping and Klaus grabs it and tries to strangle it. The cat fights for its life, cutting Klaus's hands and face. The boy thinks he hears the bones of the cat breaking and begins to wail himself. A young woman who has taken her lover around the corner for a kiss sees Klaus squatting over the animal and runs to him, screaming, "What are you doing? You brutal boy! Stop it now!" The boyfriend grabs Klaus by the shirt, pulling him away from his victim, and the woman crouches over the animal and takes it into her arms. "The poor thing is still alive," she whispers, and when the man turns to look, Klaus tears out of his grip and runs. Before he reaches home, he is caught in a cloudburst that soaks him to the skin. Without waking his family, he goes to his room, hides the wet pajamas under his bed, and sleeps. The next morning he has a raging fever. The maid finds the wet clothes and shows them to the boy's puzzled mother, but by this time Klaus is delirious, and a doctor is called. In a fever dream he sees his body burn from the toes up. His legs turn to ashes, leaving two large black spots on the bed. The child begins a confession. My mouth, he thinks, I must tell it before my mouth burns. The mother, who is sitting beside the bed, sees her son sit bolt upright and begin to speak. He confesses all, both the real and the imagined: the dangling Dieter, the hole in the sheet, the blinded dog, the hidden spoons, the cat. His mother doesn't understand a word. She stares at his cut face and tries to get him to lie down, but he pushes her away. She wipes his forehead with a cold cloth and makes soothing noises. The boy keeps looking at the door. He hears his father coming up the stairs, dragging his foot behind him. The sound beats in his ears, but his father doesn't appear. Klaus is on fire and he screams the words "brutal boy" over and over until the doctor arrives and sedates him. Klaus sleeps, and when he wakes, his throat is sore but the fever has broken. "Am I alive?" he asks his mother. After she assures him that he is, he sleeps again. Klaus recovers and finds that he is free of the wicked thoughts and has no desire to roam the city. His cure seems absolute. But in the novella's last scene, Klaus is sitting in the parlor on a Sunday with his parents and several aged relatives. He has endured the rigors of a starched collar and a long church service. He looks at his great-uncle Frederick, a wizened little man with a concave chest and arms and legs like sticks. The old man falls asleep with his mouth open and Klaus begins to daydream. He climbs onto his uncle's lap and blows air into the gaping mouth until the octogenarian blows up like a balloon and floats over the heads of the company, enormous and weightless. Then he bursts. Bones, skin, teeth, fingers, toes, and old tobacoo juice rain down on the party. Klaus smiles and turns his attention to chubby Aunt Lotte, eyeing her

big ankles with interest. The story ends with Klaus muttering to himself, "One times two is two. Two times two
are four, three times two are six . . ."

I snapped the book shut and looked out my window.
The snow had stopped. It's an odd little work, I thought,
slight and strange but good enough to translate, a gruesome
comedy really. I began the next morning, searching for
English words to mirror the German, and the effort
changed the story for me. As I transcribed Klaus's fantasies,
I had an uncanny feeling of intimacy. Brief but vague memories surfaced and then were gone. I was in the Webster
Municipal Library, standing beside another little girl I
didn't know. It was hot. She had a red face. It must have
been summer. I wanted to shake her. That was all. I remembered nothing else, but the vision was provocative
and brought with it a feeling of mild distress. To the extent
that my text grew, the German one disappeared, and I
claimed the new narrative. It's mine, I said to myself, my
reinvention. I'm making it. And so I struggled over the
sentences, polishing them until they seemed perfect, and
I recall that once when I paused from the translation to
go to the bathroom, I caught a glimpse of myself in the
mirror and was taken aback. I was grinning like a half-wit.
Good God, I thought, you don't even look like yourself.

By the time I met with Professor Rose again, I had done
twenty pages out of ninety-five. When I handed him the
manuscript, I had to hide my anticipation. He took the
draft and began to read. I examined his expression carefully, looking for the sign of approval I hoped for, but his
face was impassive. He turned the page. The room was
overheated and I took off my sweater. He turned another

page. The corners of his mouth fell. He hates it, I thought. The professor was wearing corduroys and the knees were worn. I looked at those knees and clenched my jaw. Finally he looked up at me.

"You've taken liberties," he said.

"I have?" My disappointment must have been apparent.

"It's good," he said quickly, "really very good, but it's changed."

"Is it?" I said. "Where?"

Professor Rose gave me a shrewd glance, as if he didn't believe me. "The tone," he said. "You've missed the tone."

"The tone! That's what I was most careful about." I dug out the little green volume from my bag, opened it to *The Brutal Boy*, and scanned the first paragraph. I looked up at him. He was smiling.

"Did you like the story, Miss Vegan?"

"I think so," I said. "I'm not sure 'like' is the right word. I laughed when I read it, but I found it a little perverse at the same time."

He nodded but said nothing more. His eyes were bright, knowing. He looked like a man with a secret.

"Frankly," I went on, my voice defensive, "I'm not sure whether it's any good or not, whether it's just an exercise in sublimated sadism or something more than that. As for the tone, I think I got it."

"Do you like Klaus?" he said to me, leaning forward over his desk.

This second bald question caught me off guard. He held his eyes on mine, and the directness of his gaze startled me. My abdomen tightened. I crossed my legs. His expression was wry, almost smug, and despite my discomfort, I looked at him, drawn by what he seemed to know but wouldn't say. I dropped my eyes. "Why do you say that?" I mumbled the words. "What do you mean?"

"Just what I said. Do you like him?"

"Is that pertinent?"

"To what?"

"To the translation. Whether I like him or not. What difference does it make?"

"It could make a great deal of difference, don't you thnk? To the tone of the narration I was speaking of earlier, to how we finally remake the story in English."

"Well," I said. "I don't know if I like him, Professor Rose. I just don't know." I spat out the words.

The professor raised his eyebrows. "Good enough," he said, smiling at my vehemence. "We have time. We'll uncover it slowly, get down to it. Keep going, and we'll talk next week."

"What about the tone?" I said.

He waved a hand in the air. "Oh, you'll get it," he said, and with that, I was dismissed.

This conversation, during which very little was said, spawned innumerable dialogues I invented as I lay in bed. I argued with Professor Rose and explained myself. He was wrong about the tone. I knew. I understood Klaus. I had entered the story completely. The new words I chose were never haphazard. Couldn't he hear the music of the language I was giving to the boy? I saw the professor's green eyes. What do you know? I thought. What do you see? Old men think they own the truth. And so I fought him when he wasn't there. Alone, I was strident and articulate in a way I could never be when I faced him. His presence made me shrink, and though it irritated me, I also looked

forward to that sensation of being dwarfed, couldn't wait
to sit beside him in his office again. In my solitude, these
conflicting impulses were positively boisterous. I careened
from one to the other, a rebel one minute, meek the next,
a crusader who turned to jelly. It wore me out. Had I
known how long this war would continue, I might have
negotiated a truce, but the future was an enigma.

The Brutal Boy grew in English. I worked hard all week.
By now Klaus was moving through the house touching
things, his stealthy fingers exploring taboo anatomies, and
the words I found for him excited me. Every room he
enters becomes a site of secret knowledge, every object a
treasure because he has handled it. I saw the house too,
every detail, even though Krüger leaves much unsaid. The
image of this house was stolen from somewhere, but where?
Klaus picks up a figurine—a girl with a goose. It was
familiar to me. The boy strokes the porcelain dress, the
shoes. He turns her upside down. Writing the scene, I felt
breathless, agitated, and had to stop. For the rest of that
week I translated nothing more, but I had already done
fifteen new pages. On the morning of my appointment
with Professor Rose, I changed my clothes several times,
choosing in the end a skirt and small sweater. I'll provoke
him, I thought. Serves him right.

The professor gave me a fast, hard glance when I entered
the room, motioned for me to sit down, and handed me
an edited version of my earlier pages. The manuscript was
covered with slashes and notes in the margin. I felt my
face redden in misery. Without looking at him, I gave him
the new work.

"Would you go over those pages for next week?" he said.

I didn't answer him.

"Don't worry, Miss Vegan," he said, his voice tight with formality. "It's not as extensive as it appears."

His tone of voice wounded me, struck me as a fresh betrayal, and I looked at the floor, intent on hiding the pain in my face.

He was reading, his gray head bent over the typed pages, his mouth set in a tense grimace. Screw you, I thought to myself, Mr. Know-It-All. I listened to the sound of his pen. He coughed once. Then, out of nowhere, he snorted. I looked at him. He was staring at my feet. "Good heavens, girl!" he shouted at the feet. "It's cold outside! Don't you freeze in those ridiculous shoes? Where are your galoshes?"

I didn't know what to say. Had he been anyone else, I would have howled with laughter, but the man was angry. I glared at him.

The outburst was already over. He returned to his reading as if he had never spoken. I looked at him and folded my arms. Then I had a powerful urge to climb up on his desk and start singing. I can't sing, but that was beside the point. I imagined myself belting out a song in a big voice from his desktop and stripping. I saw myself pull off my sweater and throw it at his head. I smiled.

He raised his eyes from the page. "This looks better," he said. "I think you're finding it."

"What?" I said. It was a curt, rude response.

He gazed at me and pressed his index finger into the hollow beneath his cheekbone. Then he nodded. It was the nod that unraveled me, with its suggestion of penetration, almost telepathy. I looked back at him and felt my jaw relax, my lips part. Who are you? I thought. He took in my whole face with a leisure that astounded me. We looked at each other too long, and the impropriety made

me tremble. My question was forgotten. He blinked, took
a breath, and collected himself. His sharp gaze clouded
and his face changed. I nearly spoke then, but I felt only
sound in my throat, no words.

"Perhaps this is a mistake," he said. "The story, you
know." He seemed to be addressing a third person in the
room. "It's a Pandora's box of sorts, isn't it?" His voice was
soft. He doesn't want anyone to hear us, I thought. Then
he spoke more loudly. "How old are you, Miss Vegan?"

"I'm twenty-two."

He nodded, running a hand through his hair. "I see,"
he said. This information appeared to make him sad.

"Professor Rose?" I didn't know what I was going to say,
but I would have spoken had he not ignored me.

"I think that's enough for today," he said. He gave me
a bewildered look.

I gathered my books and left, closing the door behind
me. In the hallway, I heard him muttering to himself. The
words were indistinct but came quickly, easily, as if he
knew them by heart. He's quoting something, I thought.
I wished I were alone in the hall so I could press my ear
to the keyhole and listen.

That evening I sat down to work on the novella again.
The boy is leaving the house. The passage was troubling.
I rewrote it several times. He pulls on the heavy door,
dreading noise, feels the night air, and slips out into the
street. I changed the verbs, the adjectives. Each time I did
it over, I saw Klaus going through the door into the street.
I looked up from the book and my mind wandered. I
remembered a white nightgown my mother gave me when
I was seven. I had forgotten it. Then I imagined myself
pushing open the door to my parents' house and stepping

outside. I felt my bare feet on wet grass. I saw the lights
from Webster a mile away. Wee Willie Winkie runs
through the town, I thought. Upstairs and downstairs. In
the fantasy I peeked into a window but then stopped myself. Don't look. Go home. I remembered the sound of
Professor Rose's voice from the other side of the door. I
bent down to hear the words, but they were monstrous,
and I suppressed the daydream. Then I spoke sternly to
myself. Keep your distance, I said, your sense of irony.
You're losing your grip, confusing one thing with another.
Buck up. This little speech was an attempt to save myself
from what had, in effect, already happened.

   During the meetings that followed, Professor Rose
scarcely looked at me. The novella was the exclusive site
of our communication. Little Klaus became a go-between.
When we sat side by side on Thursdays, and I watched
his pen move across my pages and listened to his criticisms,
I was invariably gripped by a nameless excitement and
anxiety. His violent editing of my translation left me feeling
battered but not unhappy. I could see that he was usually
right, and my admiration made me humble. It was clear
to me that the professor loved the story, and when he
mentioned Klaus, his voice would often break in tenderness. His German was perfect, as nuanced and beautiful
as his English, and I sometimes wondered why he had let
me touch the story at all. He was also extremely possessive
of the text and presumed a knowledge of the author's intent
that confounded me. In a single mad moment I actually
suspected him of having written it. But I had the little book
in front of me, complete with copyright page, and my doubt
shamed me. Still, his relation to The Brutal Boy was oddly
personal and his opinions about it absolute. Once, during

a session, he roared at me about a paragraph I had mis-
translated. "This is a passage of great sexual tension, Miss
Vegan. Erotic power—latent, of course, but there! You've
left it all out, made it bland! My God, girl, look here. It's
loins, not limbs. Where did you get limbs? *Lende!* There's
a great difference, don't you think, between looking at loins
and looking at limbs? Do you want to denature the entire
work?" I stared down at the page and uttered an apology.
Then I turned to look at him. His eyes were keen. He didn't
smile, but I thought I detected faint humor in his glance.
"Get your anatomy straight next time," he said. "Yes sir,"
I replied, and we returned to the page. It is impossible for
me to say why this scolding made me feel loved, but it
did. The heart is unfathomable.

The winter was short, the spring long that year. My life
continued to be punctuated by Thursdays with Professor
Rose, during which nothing and everything happened. And
I was slowly making my way toward Klaus's last vindictive
daydream. There were others in my life too, and I saw a
lot of Ruth. Although I didn't tell her about the professor,
we shared everything else, which basically came down to
books and men. Ruth liked to call the boys who came
around "suitors." It was a grand word that summoned both
Homer and Austen, and using it lent a kind of artificial
formality to the disorder of "dating." Those young men
were a mixed lot, but they were plentiful—a little more
so for me than for Ruth—and the fact is, I don't remember
all of them. The warm weather made the boys eager. They
were all in search of an object, and some of them believed
I was it. Their styles varied, but there was often some sort

of hesitation or scuffle at the door. The daring ones attacked
me bodily, grabbing me in the hallway outside my apartment and planting big wet kisses on my lips. One student
who had lectured me soberly on Kierkegaard all through
dinner actually picked me up off the ground as he made
his move on the sidewalk outside my building. The action
so startled me I had to throttle a laugh. Others were timid,
hemming and hawing at an evening's end, looking at me
expectantly, waiting for an invitation to stay. Stanley was
among the shy ones, an Orthodox Jew who lived with his
parents in Riverdale and studied Renaissance literature. We
had long talks on the steps of Low Library in the sunshine
before we had our single dinner date. I suppose Stanley
fell in love with me during those talks about life and books,
but he probably loved someone else, a person who wasn't
me. His tiny mannerisms and careful conversation made
me feel large, bold, almost crude when I was beside him.
Irreverent jokes, sexual innuendo, and a general zest for
things forbidden poured out of me in his presence. I
couldn't help myself. Stanley seemed to enjoy my patter,
and the truth is, I liked him. We had Chinese food, and
while we ate, I noticed he was trembling, but we talked
and drank beer and laughed and his hands stopped shaking. After he walked me home, he kissed me at the door.
His face was flushed, and from so close, his features were
delicate and lovely. I asked him to come in, but at the last
minute he fled and never called again. It probably was for
the best. My attraction to Stanley was short-lived. I think
I wanted him because he never pushed me. That was the
problem with most of the boys. Their intense wishes made
me claustrophobic. They were always breathing on me,
pulling, tugging, even begging for some mysterious gift

they thought I could give them. But I didn't really have it—the thing they wanted. I know they dreamed of sexual triumph, of some erotic cataclysm that would erase their need, and I know that by eluding them I became more and more a creature of their hopes, a vaporous being with blond hair and blue eyes. They weren't to blame. Distortion is part of desire. We always change the things we want.

Late that spring my life changed in three decisive ways. I ran out of money, Ruth fell in love, and Paris popped up again. May was a beautiful month—clear, warm weeks that made me ache with restlessness—and I would have liked to go out every night, but my stipend was quickly coming to an end. I hadn't paid the rent for May and I lived in fear of a visit from Mr. Then, my landlord who lived in New Jersey. That was his real name: Mr. Louis Then. I'd never seen him, but his spectral name was horribly apt to my predicament, calling to mind the already gone, the past due. I began to refuse dinners in restaurants when I knew I would have to pay, and subsisted on a diet of noodles and eggs. My weight dropped. I needed new shoes but couldn't afford them. Now I find it incomprehensible that I didn't turn to my parents for help. They had very little money, it's true, but they would have gladly given me enough for shoes. I couldn't bring myself to ask them. Asking would have been an admission of hardship, not only to them but to myself, and I was stubborn. Although my shoes had holes in the bottom, the rest of me was never shabby. In fact, I noticed that students much richer than I was often affected poverty, wearing torn jeans and ragged shirts. Unlike them, I was always pressed and neat and

very careful with my clothes. I hid my true straits even
from Ruth, although she guessed and paid for more meals
than she should have and brought me gifts she pretended
weren't charity. Ruth's parents sent her money every month
and she shared with me. I loved her for it, even though
the indebtedness pained me. That was before she met Robert Cohen and disappeared in a cloud of love. He was in
advertising, of all things, but as Ruth said—rather defen-
sively, I thought—he loved Wittgenstein. My friend was
rarely at home, and when I did reach her, she was full of
news about the remarkable Mr. Cohen. I was jealous, I
suppose, and withdrew rather than confront her. But I
missed Ruth terribly, and I understood once she was gone
how much her presence colored mine. Ruth was the heroine of her own life story, and when we were together,
she made me the heroine of mine. She gave daily hardships
the stature of romance or drama. Once when a mutual
friend asked about my apartment, and I reported it was
small and dark, Ruth laughed and said, "David, it's a rat-
infested hovel, a student garret, just awful, but wonderful."
She meant it. In the middle of the month, I returned home
one evening to discover that a mouse had broken into a
package of macaroni, leaving his tiny turds all over my
dinner, and as I rinsed off the noodles under the faucet, I
started to cry. I cried through the entire meal and didn't
stop until I had washed and put away the last dish.

Just around the same time, I ended up at a dinner party
where Paris was one of the guests. Tim, a handsome, phleg-
matic boy from my linguistics and philosophy class had
invited me. I went, tempted most by the idea of a large

meal. I remember that the dinner was held in a big ruin of a loft on White Street, that it was given by a painter named Sam who had turned all his canvases to the wall for the occasion, that his girlfriend was beautiful and silent, and that two of the other guests, Jonathan and Rita, were introduced to me as "a performance team." "They work with objects," Sam explained, but I never found out what this meant, and throughout the party, I had occasional visions of the two as jugglers. Paris arrived last, wearing a deep pink suit, and when I saw him coming through the door, I felt a spasm of discomfort. But he greeted me like an old friend.

"Iris, Iris, Iris, how are you?" He moved close to my face. "You look pale. Are you all right? Is the city disagreeing with you?"

"I'm just fine," I said. "This is Tim." I took my friend's arm. I don't think I'd ever touched him before. Tim smiled.

At the dinner table, Paris planted himself directly across from me. We ate pasta, a disappointment. The conversation meandered. I've forgotten most of it. There was talk of artists I didn't know, of galleries and their politics. I had three helpings of noodles and looked from one guest to another. The beautiful girlfriend, Laura, ate quickly and smoked. Tim showed himself to be well informed but delivered every comment in the same bored tone. Jonathan and Rita, however, were lively and had the same laugh. It made me wonder if years of intimacy could produce a shared tone even in a primal sound like laughter. I tried to keep my eyes off Paris, which was difficult. He demanded my attention even when he wasn't speaking to me, going so far as to lean to one side in order to keep himself in my sight. No one seemed to notice but me, and

I pretended indifference. Then Paris brought up the painting. I had lost track of the conversation, but the name brought me back. " 'The Tempest,' " Paris was saying, "by Giorgione. It's better than anything."

I looked Paris in the face. "You're right. I've never been to Venice, but I know it from reproductions. It must be three years since I've looked at it, but it made a huge impression on me. I remember it well."

Rita said, "It's the one with the woman and the storm?"

Paris nodded without turning to look at her. He stared at me. "You have a good memory for paintings?"

"I do, especially that one."

"Could you describe it now?"

"Is this a test?"

Everyone at the table was silent.

"No, I'm really curious, interested . . ."

"Go ahead, Iris," Tim said. "If I've seen it, I don't remember it."

"Well," I said, conscious that all six were listening. I looked at nobody, focusing on the backside of one of Sam's canvases. "There's a woman sitting on a riverbank in the foreground to the right. She's nursing a child—not a tiny infant, a baby who also sits on the ground. One of her arms rests on the child's shoulder, I think, and the other is on her knee. She's naked, except for a cloth draped around her shoulders." I closed my eyes to see it better, to remember it exactly. "Her right breast is exposed, the one the baby sucks. Her body is turned sideways, but she's looking up, her eyes lifted, staring straight out of the painting, and her face, her expression is . . ." I shook my head. "It's calm, remote, but you feel that she's looked up for one instant and seen you, and that that single second is forever." I stammered over the last phrase, embarrassed by the emotion I felt. No one said a word. I went on. "The most delicate foliage grows in front of her, and it makes a pattern on the pale skin of her leg without hiding its shape. There's a tall tree behind her, lush but narrow, and other trees to the left, also young and thin. Behind her is a bridge and the buildings of a city, but they look dead and un-inhabited for some reason. And then there's the storm with dark clouds above and an exquisite bolt of lightning which gives the painting its curious illumination. It's not real light but a kind of inner light, the light of strong memories. I can't explain it, but even while you look at that painting, you feel that it's already past, that you've already seen it. Maybe that's why it has such a powerful effect afterward. I mean, the thing itself is memory, is an afterlife, and so you're remembering a memory . . . " I coughed, put my hand to my mouth, and looked down. I'm sure I blushed.

Tim spoke first. "That's amazing."

"You're finished?" Paris said.

I nodded.

"Haven't you forgotten something?"

"Have I?"

"What?" said Jonathan. "She was so specific."

"Yes, she was, wasn't she?" Paris said. He tapped his fork against his plate three times.

I looked at Sam. "You know that painting, don't you? What did I leave out?"

"There's a man in the painting." Paris answered for Sam.

Sam nodded.

"I can't believe it," I said. "Where is he? Way in the back somewhere?"

Sam looked at me. "No, he's in the foreground far to

the left, looking in the direction of the woman. What's so strange is that you remembered details that had slipped my mind completely—the way she sits, the cloth, the trees . . ."

"I thought I remembered it exactly," I said.

"You did," Paris said.

"I blanked out a whole person."

"Because you entered the painting so completely."

"What do you mean, Paris?" Rita craned her neck to see him.

I noticed that Laura had her elbows on the table and was resting her chin in her hands. She looked directly at me.

"You became the man," Paris said. "You stepped into his shoes and promptly deleted him from the painting. He's a spectator, too, almost a double of the person viewing the picture. For you he was expendable. You saw him but didn't see him."

I tried to conjure the missing man.

"I don't know about that, Paris," said Jonathan. "People forget all kinds of things."

I couldn't remember him at all.

"Not a person who can recall a work of art as well as that." Paris smiled.

"Are you saying it's natural to forget the man?" Rita asked Paris.

"In this case it was natural, natural to Iris."

His comment caused a tiny contraction in my chest. Then it passed. I watched Paris. He was hitting the plate with his fork again.

"Is that art criticism or psychoanalysis?" said Tim.

"A bit of both." Paris flashed a wide grin across the table.

"You and Iris are close friends?" Laura said this loudly.

Paris looked sharply to his left and stared at her for a couple of seconds. "My God," he said. "She talks, too."

Laura looked down at her plate, flustered. I saw her right eye, cheek, and upper lip convulse in a tic. Then it happened again. Rita, who was sitting beside Laura, turned toward her. No one spoke. Sam gave Paris a look of reproach and I felt the tension of anger in my shoulders and neck. "We hardly know each other." I spoke in a big voice, looking straight at Laura. "But that's hardly a deterrent for Paris. One look is enough for him. He'll tell you all about yourself after two minutes of conversation, and I doubt whether it ever occurs to him that he's terribly deluded." I thought I would say more, but I stopped.

Paris stabbed himself with an imaginary knife.

"Laura," Sam said, putting his hand on her arm. Then he lowered his voice.

Paris leaned across the table and smiled at me. "You're a pistol," he said. "I like that. And besides, I deserved it."

I made a face at him. But his words toppled my certainty. He's always shifting, I thought, moving out of my reach.

The party ended soon after that, and I continued to reconstruct the painting in my mind, trying to produce the lost man, but I had no luck. I thanked Sam and said goodbye to the other guests. I waved at Paris, who was speaking to Laura, and he rushed over to me.

"I'll send you a reproduction tomorrow," he said.

"I can look it up, Paris."

"No need. I'll send it by messenger. But you should give me your address."

I felt Tim beside me, the sleeve of his coat touching mine.

"Really, you don't have to go to all that trouble."

He put his mouth near my ear. "You should see it, you know, see him." He made the word "him" emphatic, and I withdrew.

I wrote my address on a small piece of paper with my phone number and handed it to him. It wasn't a casual act. Scribbling the letters and numbers, I was aware of my own deliberateness. Paris took the paper from my hand and put it carefully into his wallet.

Tim paid for a taxi back to the Upper West Side. "That Paris," he said, "is a weird little guy. What a suit!"

"Maybe," I said, "but he's no idiot." I had spoken sharply, and my tone took me by surprise. I was defending Paris.

I softened my voice. "Of course, you're right. He doesn't look like anybody else."

The messenger was deaf. He must have felt the vibrations of the buzzer, because he came in without any problem. I signed the paper he handed me and motioned a thank-you, pulling a book from the padded envelope: *Painting in Italy: 1500–1600*. Paris had marked the page with a note. "Here it is. Sorry it's black and white—the best I could do. The real question is: Who is this guy?" The man was standing in the left corner of the painting holding a staff. I looked at him for a long time. He wasn't familiar to me. It was like seeing him for the first time, and yet everything else was just as I had remembered it. But where had he disappeared to? How many others are there? I thought. People, things, seen and then forgotten, leaving nothing behind them, not even the knowledge that they're missing. I stared down at the painting and into the mild eyes of the woman and then at her raised leg and the leaves that appeared to mark her flesh with their design.

o

The last two weeks of school, I managed to live on next
to nothing. A twenty-dollar bill remained in my wallet.
Until I found work, I promised myself, I wouldn't break
it. A box of rice, six eggs, and two packages of spaghetti
made dinners. I went from one restaurant to another on
upper Broadway asking for a waitressing job. They had no
openings. I was dogged, repeating the same question in
the same dead voice, listening for the rejection, and going
back into the street. There's a kind of desperation people
don't feel and don't bother to reflect on. That was the case
with me. Now I pity that girl pounding the pavement, but
when I did it, I had the emotions of a rock. Poverty made
me stupid. I spent a lot of time thinking about beautiful
shoes, choosing the ones I wanted in a window and then
changing my mind. This game kept me occupied, and at
first I played it without remorse and without envy for the
young women who actually entered the stores, but with
each day my desire escalated. Shoes were out of the question. I began to lust after the useless trinkets vendors sold
on the street, and the day before I was to see Professor
Rose for the last time that spring, I succumbed and bought
a comb for my hair, paying for it with the twenty-dollar
bill—imitation tortoiseshell with gold trim. It cost three
dollars. The purchase was a folly, and I berated myself. It
wasn't the comb I wanted, it was the exchange, the act of
parting with money. For a few minutes it brought me a
sense of freedom.

I finished *The Brutal Boy* that night. Poor bloated Uncle
Frederick hovers near the chandelier and then goes to
pieces. This time the ending made me sad, but I liked the

feeling. Tomorrow, I said to myself, I will speak to Professor Rose. I worked on a speech. What I finally came up with, however, was so tepid and veiled that only a clairvoyant would have been able to read any passion in it. Still, every time I rehearsed the words, I lost my breath and gasped for air. By the next morning I was a shuddering wreck of expectation, flying around my apartment like a wounded bird. I wore the comb. My hope made me pathetic, but I comforted myself with the fact that I was my only witness.

Outside Professor Rose's office, I breathed deeply before I knocked, and then at the sound of his voice I went in. He didn't look up. His head was bent over some papers on his desk. I hesitated and began. "Professor Rose, I've wanted to tell you for a long time how much it has meant for me to work with you . . ."

He looked up, his expression kind. "I'm sorry, Miss Vegan," he said. "What did you say? I've been buried in this dissertation, can't make head or tail of it. It's pure gibberish as far as I can tell . . ."

I forgot my lines.

"What were you saying, Miss Vegan?"

"Please call me Iris," I said, my voice faltering. "I'd like you to call me Iris." It had all gone wrong.

"All right, Iris," he said, eyeing me with vague amusement.

"I have the whole manuscript," I said. "It's all retyped." There was a hysterical note in my voice that worried me. What was I doing? My stomach made a loud noise. I had skipped dinner the night before and breakfast that morning as penance for the comb. The noise came again, a long rumble.

Professor Rose raised his eyebrows, and one corner of his mouth moved.

I sniffed. I was going to cry. Don't do it, I said to myself. Don't do it.

"Iris," my teacher said. "Look at me. Are you okay?"

I took one look at his sympathetic face and started bawling in earnest.

He waved his hands in the air, repeating a gesture something like an unfinished clap. "Good grief," he said. "What is the matter?"

"I don't know," I wailed, honking into a tissue he had given me.

"Have you eaten breakfast?"

I shook my head.

"Let's get you something to eat then." He stood up and grabbed his jacket that was hanging over the back of a chair.

Professor Rose bought me bacon and eggs at Tom's Restaurant on Broadway and 113th. He watched soberly as I wolfed down my food. I ate everything, scraping up the last specks of egg with my toast.

"You were hungry," he said to me.

"I have a big appetite in the morning," I said, avoiding his eyes.

He didn't say anything to this, and we sat in silence. Then he said, "The university gives emergency loans. Did you know that?"

My face turned hot. I gazed at a woman across from us who was speaking very softly to a large paper bag on the seat next to her. She had bought only coffee. As she spoke to the bag, she stuffed little packages of sugar into her pockets. I looked down at the Formica surface of the table.

Professor Rose reached inside his jacket and retrieved a wallet.

"No," I said to him. "Please." I put up my hands as if I were warding off a blow.

"Iris," he said. "As your friend."

"Please, you don't understand. I can't pay you back. I don't even have a job yet."

"It's not a loan." His voice was soft.

"I can't," I said, shaking my head hard.

He pushed four twenty-dollar bills across the table. I stared at the money. With it, I could put off Mr. Then. It was sickening to want it so much. "No," I said. A sharp pain in my stomach made me shift in the booth.

"Take it," he said.

I didn't touch the money. I lifted my face to his. "I'll miss you," I said, "this summer. There won't be anyone to yell at me. I'll come and visit you in the fall."

"I won't be here in the fall. I'm going to North Carolina. I thought you knew that."

I knew nothing.

"Thank you very much for breakfast," I said. "It's the best breakfast I've had in a long time." I stood up. My stomach hurt.

Professor Rose took the money back, but when we were standing near the door ready to leave, he slipped the bills into my pocket. He did it with the deftness of a thief, and I admired his agility. It betrayed a side of him I didn't know and couldn't have foreseen. I kept the eighty dollars. It would save me.

Standing outside Tom's, I looked at him, at his face and hair, at his shoulders in the thin jacket, and I resisted the desire to touch him, to move close to him and put my face to his neck. He looked back at me and shook his head, smiling.

"What are you thinking?" I said to him. I felt better in the air. There was a wind and it hit my face, blowing my hair out behind me.

He didn't reply. "Listen to me," he said. "Go to Low Library and get yourself an emergency loan. You should be able to get three hundred dollars. Do it now."

I nodded.

"Goodbye. I'll see you when I get back." He turned fast without giving me his hand and walked away. I watched him leave and then started in the opposite direction. I had gone half a block before I remembered the translation. I ran after him and screamed, "Stop! Stop!" He didn't hear me. I caught up with him and reached for his arm. He spun around, and I saw a savage face, lined and contorted with emotion. His expression shocked me, and I think I stepped back from him, apologizing without knowing why. "I'm sorry but you forgot this. I wouldn't know where to send it." I handed him the manuscript.

He took it with his left hand, and with his free hand he took mine. It wasn't a handshake. He squeezed my fingers until the bones hurt, looking at me, his mouth set grimly, his eyes steady. Then he let go.

I opened my mouth to speak, but he shook his head and put a finger close to my lips. For a second time, he turned and left me, but that last time, I could see an urgency in his step that hadn't been there before.

o

A year and a half went by before I saw Professor Rose again. I kept the memory of our parting safe, hoarding it as a sign of unspoken feeling. All summer long, I talked to his ghost, telling the shadow what I had wanted to tell the man. For the next three months I fended for myself, working three part-time jobs—as a swimming instructor at the YMCA, a floor model at Bloomingdale's, and a waitress in a SoHo bar. I liked the swimmers, and the hours I spent with them in the echo chamber of the ancient pool in midtown was a respite from the world. They flapped and puffed and tried hard as I held them one at a time, guiding them through the shallow water. Twice a week I strolled the floors of Bloomingdale's in a ridiculous getup made from parachute silk—a screaming red jumpsuit, tight and airless, with six zippers. The result of one man's futuristic fantasies, it wasn't intended to give dignity to the wearer, but I suffered it for twenty dollars an hour, and whenever I had the chance, I sneaked off to the ladies' room and read novels in a stall. But most of my money was made at Rudy's, a pretentious little wine bar on West Broadway that served old salads and soft cheeses to an expensive clientele, and where the uniformly pretty waitresses discussed the finer points of cocaine, Quaaludes, and other intoxicants, arguing for this one or that, with the energy of young philosophers. My fellow workers read my silence on the subject as moral condemnation, but in truth, I've always been afraid of drugs. The jolts and tingles that might be gained from these substances don't attract me. My interest has always been in maintaining balance, not tipping it. Untampered with, my system was already difficult, queasy, on the edge. It didn't crave interference. Still, I envied those girls their fun, their resilience. They worked hard but were indifferent, shrugging off the nastiness of the customers—their impatience, rudeness, vile sexual jokes. They had a light touch. I, on the other hand, slogged through it, turning rigid at every leer and comment, fighting the urge to retort in kind or dump a glass of Chardonnay over a well-groomed head, and by the end of the night, I felt bumped and bruised. Not once did I consider leaving, however. I needed the job to pay the rent and felt lucky to have it.

One night I looked up and saw Paris sitting at a table near the window. It was late and he was alone. Seeing him made me jump. For me, I thought, he's a creature of superstition. I have to get over it. He's never done anything to me. In fact, I rather like him. I walked over to the table and Paris smiled at me, but he seemed less cheerful than before, and I realized I preferred him that way.

"Did you get the book?" he whispered loudly.

"Yes," I whispered back. "But I don't have your address or number, so I couldn't thank you. Thank you."

He signaled me to move closer. "You saw *him* this time?" he said.

"I did," I said aloud.

Paris pretended our conversation was secret, moving his eyes back and forth in an exaggerated way. "Shhhh!" he said. "You wouldn't want them to know."

I smiled and shook my head. "It's that serious, is it?"

"Absolutely."

Paris stayed until I had finished work, and we walked down the street to La Gammelle and shared a bottle of wine. He didn't exactly tell me the story of his life that night. When I left him, I knew little more than when we first sat down, but he mentioned his mother and a sister and the town in New Jersey where he had grown up. It may have been conscious on his part, but these details grounded him and relieved me of the impression that he had sprung from nowhere fully grown, in a brightly colored suit. During our conversation, Paris leaned across the table often and gestured significantly, only rarely taking his eyes off mine.

"You're not like other people," he said to me after a pause.

"But I think I am like other people in most ways."

"No," he said. "You can fly."

I stared at him. "All I have to do is flap my wings, right?"

Paris nodded at me very slowly. "That's it." He didn't smile and there was no irony in his face.

"I have no idea what you're talking about," I said.

"Often words have to sink in, you know, go underground for a while."

A crowd had gathered at the bar, and I overheard a woman say, "I couldn't take it anymore. He just went nuts, walking around the kitchen in his underwear talking to himself like I wasn't there . . . " Doesn't seem that serious, I thought to myself. Paris said nothing more about flying, but we talked on, and just before I was about to say good-bye, he asked me to go to Los Angeles with him for a month. He had the money to take me, no strings attached. My obligations in New York were minimal. I had three "crummy" jobs that would be easy to leave. At first I thought he was joking, but he wasn't. I said no to him, and he seemed to accept the rejection in good humor. When we parted, he gave me one of those European kisses that don't land. That night I lay in bed and thought about him, imagining his hotel somewhere in Beverly Hills, and in my mind it was a cliché of luxury: powder-blue walls, heavy curtains, and in the bathroom, the fixtures were gleaming brass. I slept deeply all night but just before I opened my eyes in the morning, I had a tiny dream or half-wakeful vision. A small brown sparrow flew right into my face.

In the middle of June I was robbed. It was a phantom robbery, as it turned out, because I had nothing to steal: no television, no stereo, no money hidden under the mattress. I didn't even own a typewriter at that point. I came home to an open door, an open window, and a mess. That was all. I picked up my clothes and books and spent the money I had been saving for a dress on a police lock. A week later, a young architecture student named Louise Hartwig was raped in the elevator by a man wearing a ski mask on a ninety-degree day. The police questioned everyone in the building, but as far as I know, they never found the man who hurt her. She left the city. Her father came to get her things. I saw him carrying boxes of books out to a station wagon parked in front of the building. It must have been her father. She looked like him. I remember that when I passed him in the lobby, I studied his face briefly, expecting to see some sign of his suffering, but he seemed only tired.

Not long after the rape, I started wearing the suit. Ruth had never reclaimed it. It was one of those all-season weights, a very thin wool, which made it a little hot but bearable. After work I would change into this disguise and take the subway home. I wore the hat, too, tucking my hair underneath it. My cohorts at Rudy's teased me about this new habit, but I had a reasonable explanation. "No one bothers me," I would say. "In the dark, people think I'm a man." I remember coming out of the toilet one night in the suit and meeting Izzy, another waitress. She put her hands on her hips and looked me up and down. "You're looney, Iris," she said. "Crazy, I mean it." I walked past her. Then she called after me, "One weird chick!" I turned my head. "Isabel," I said. "Stuff it up your ass."

This remark, of absolutely no interest in itself, was extraordinary to me. I had never said those words before. The insult had come easily, naturally, and standing outside Rudy's, I thought: It's the suit. The clothes were more than armor. They transformed me. Another person had leapt forward and spoken. I pulled the fedora down close to my eyes, put my hands deep in my pockets, and started off down the street, whistling. I never whistled. I'm a new man, I thought to myself, and laughed out loud. My wandering began that same night and lasted all summer. I walked and walked, from one neighborhood to another, looking at everyone and everything, indulging myself in long stares. New York City is never quiet. There are corners of stillness, streets empty for minutes at a time, but then the peace ends. People chatter, sing, cry out. A rat runs into hiding. Once, I saw a man bring his car to a screeching stop and push a woman out the door. She was hysterical and pounded on the window, her voice hoarse from yelling. He drove away, and seeing him go, she clutched her belly like a person who had been punched, and then walked away, unsteady in her high heels. On my walks I witnessed many small scenes of love, hate, and indifference. My intention was to watch only, to keep myself at a distance, but this wasn't always possible. A young woman approached me late on a Thursday night. Bleecker Street was crowded, and she came toward me. I guessed that she wanted directions, but she took my hand and said, "Do you know what she did?" "No," I said. The girl was short and wore thick glasses. I noticed a gray shadow of dirt on her neck. "The horses," she grunted. "The bitch stole the horses." I moved backward, but she grabbed my forearm and dug her nails into my skin, snarling. "Right out of the barn." I jerked my arm away from her and headed down the street fast, relieved that she didn't pursue me. I understood then that confrontation was inevitable. It was the risk that came with every step I took, and though I didn't want to court trouble, I grew more daring as time went on, stopping in bars I wouldn't have entered alone in the past, striking up conversations with strangers I would have once avoided. People were mostly friendly and eager to talk. They told me their stories—long, rambling accounts of accidents and divorce, illness, death, money come and gone. But they didn't ask me about myself and I volunteered no information. I was Iris, the roving ear, until one night when I answered a simple question.

Below Canal Street, I had discovered a pleasant bar, Magoo's. I began to stop there immediately after work, eavesdropping while I drank one brandy. I had been there every night for a week, when the bartender leaned toward me and said, "What's your name anyway?"

I liked him. He had always left me alone, had always been respectful. I had every reason to tell him the truth. I lied. "Klaus," I said. "My name's Klaus."

"That's a funny name for a girl," he said. "German, isn't it?"

"Yes," I said. "It's short for Klausina."

He gave me a puzzled look.

"What's your name?" I said.

"Mort."

"That's nice," I said. "I like Mort."

Klaus was born in a bar, my Klaus anyway. The brutal boy found his second incarnation in me, and as soon as I took his name, I knew that from then on, the nights belonged to Klaus. In fact, he had been around for some time. The lie was a kind of truth, a birth announcement of sorts. My answer to Mort catapulted the sleeping homunculus into the world, and he woke up, a man. It never could have happened in Webster. My hometown is too small. People talk. But in the city it was easy to change my name, to be someone else. I was just another character, and not even an outlandish one. No one challenged my name or my appearance. Nevertheless, I did have a few close calls. Once, I nearly ran headlong into a group of graduate students from Columbia on Broome Street, and another time, I fled Magoo's when I saw a neighbor from 109th Street coming through the door. I was a regular at Magoo's, had befriended Mort; Fat Eddie, who was rail thin; Elise, the waitress; and Dolly, a disheveled woman with long gray hair who drank vodka only. Dolly was the one I really liked. She beat me on the back a lot and said, "You're a mixed-up kid, Klaus, but you're a cracker." To them I had confided a fictional life in bits and pieces, and the idea of being exposed was unbearable. When I saw Frank's face in the doorway, I leapt from the barstool, made an excuse, pulled my hat down to hide my face, and, passing my neighbor, heaved myself out of the door.

In early August I cut off my hair. A barber did it for five dollars, and when I came out, my hair was no more than an inch long all over my head. The barber clicked his tongue in dismay throughout the procedure, but I didn't look back. My new small head brought me a kind of steely satisfaction. I wasn't beautiful, but it didn't matter. The day of the haircut, I came home very late. After work I had gone to Magoo's and then to a strip joint called the Babydoll Lounge, where I often went to chat with one of the girls. Ramona went to business school during the day and stripped at night. Between shifts, she would often sit with me at the bar, wearing a little blue robe and her big glasses. She told me her dream was to open a toy store, and we spent time thinking up names for it. I liked the Purple Dog, but Ramona didn't. Anyway, after I said good-bye to Ramona, I wandered for a couple of hours, and it must have been three o'clock by the time I returned to my apartment. The phone rang. I thought my father was dead. I picked up the receiver expecting to hear my mother's voice. It was Paris.

"You scared me," I said. "It's so late."

"I just had this feeling you weren't asleep yet."

"You were right. How was Los Angeles? You're back, aren't you?"

"I am." He paused. "You would have liked it."

"That's very possible."

"How are things?"

I felt an involuntary compression in my throat. "Okay."

"Just okay?"

"Yes, just okay."

"You're not very talkative tonight, are you?"

"I'm tired."

"I called because I have something to tell you. I went out with some friends last night, and someone mentioned you."

"Oh?"

"He swore he saw you in some bar, a dive actually. He and some friends were 'slumming,' as the expression goes. I told him that seemed unlikely, but then he mentioned that you were wearing a suit and a hat. I remembered Halloween . . ."

I said nothing.

"Are you still there, Iris?"

"Yes."

"Aren't you going to tell me about it?"

"No." My voice was even.

Paris spoke more softly. "You don't have to, it's all right. I have an idea. You know, when you didn't come with me on the trip, I was disappointed, not so much for me but because I thought I might have been wrong about you, but then when Tony was describing you last night, it all came back to me."

"I don't know anyone named Tony." I pressed the receiver into my ear.

"He met you once or saw you once. That was enough."

I didn't answer.

"Are you there, Klaus?"

I held my breath.

"Don't worry," he was saying. "Your secret is safe with me. I wouldn't tell anyone. You're doing it now, taking off . . ."

Very slowly and carefully I put the receiver down and then took the line out of the wall. When I undressed, I said to myself, It's all over. It has to stop. The decision gave me some relief. Before I went to work the next day, I stood in front of my open closet eyeing the suit I had determined never to wear again. Then I grabbed it off the hanger and stuffed it into my bag as I had done every afternoon for weeks. I wasn't ready. To hell with Paris.

August was the longest month of the summer. The heat made the city stink, and I smelled garbage everywhere, even in my apartment. My Bloomingdale's job had come to an end, as had my work at the Y. I was left only with Rudy's. The poverty I had managed all summer threatened to become unruly. I thought about money constantly and ransacked my apartment for lost change. I remember I found three dollars and fifty-eight cents. At work we were allowed a free meal. I gorged myself so that it would last. When I roamed at night, I took to drinking Coke instead of brandy and jumped the turnstiles in the subway to save the fare. I began to stay out later and later to put off returning to my sweltering rooms. When I was home, I unplugged the phone, dreading a call from Paris, or anyone else for that matter. On several nights I walked back to 109th Street, heading north in the wee hours, letting my thoughts go here and there. It was during these walks that I filled the blanks in Klaus Krüger's life (I had given him his author's last name)—working out his narrative very carefully, trying to get the dates to correspond to some historical reality. For me Klaus remained a young man, despite the fact that those who knew me as Klaus never mistook me for a boy. The gap between what I was forced to acknowledge to the world—namely, that I was a woman—and what I dreamed inwardly didn't bother me. By becoming Klaus at night I had effectively blurred my gender. The suit, my clipped head and unadorned face altered the world's view of who I was, and I became someone else through its eyes. I even spoke differently as Klaus. I was less hesitant, used more slang, and favored colorful verbs. The midwestern accent I had worked hard to lose returned during my nocturnal wanderings, something I still find odd. The voice just came. I made no effort, and because of this, I felt my speech was neither theater nor delusion, or at least no more than any other talk is. I was that boy. Where he came from, I didn't know. Klaus had been constructed long ago in an underground place I couldn't reach.

Then I began to suffer from what can be described as perverse impulses, brief but strong desires to do something irrational. They came only at night, and only when I was Klaus. At first they didn't worry me. I've always been prone to terrible fantasies. Seeing a steep staircase, for example, instantly prompts a vision of falling. On a roof or balcony, I feel tempted to throw myself over the edge. But the wish and the act are miles apart. In Klaus that chasm shrank, and walking the streets at night, I began to feel perilously close to acting on some insane wish. Once when a man asked me for the time on Sixth Avenue, I spoke gibberish to him, the way children do when they pretend to speak Chinese. It was absurd, and I regretted it immediately. In his face I saw surprise and then a moment of fear before he hurried away. It was a warning to me, and I promised to keep myself in check. But only a couple of nights later, I passed a bum sleeping near a stoop on West End Avenue, and for no reason, I returned to examine him. His face and arms were covered with sores, his long hair lay in thick, matted sections on a filthy towel he was using as a pillow, and he stank. The smell that came from him was nauseating, horribly sweet, putrid. For a second I panicked, thinking he was dead, but I looked closely and saw his chest move evenly. I bent over him, holding my breath to shut out the stench. I stood up and felt it—a desire to kick him. It overwhelmed me. My body grew rigid and there was a tingling sensation in my foot. I remember I closed my eyes. I swayed from the waist. I forced myself to look at him again. He was abject, gruesome. Keep yourself away, I said. You'll hurt him. And then I noticed his hand. He was curled up in the fetal position with one hand over his crotch. The protective gesture made me wince. I covered my open mouth. Then I took a dollar of my tip money and tucked it into his shirt pocket. He didn't stir. The poor bastard would have slept through his own murder.

The nights enervated me. I would sleep all day, waking when it was time to go to work. I served the customers in a trance, waiting for eleven o'clock when it would start all over again. The joy I had felt in the beginning was over. The bars, the streets were a necessity now, a ritual that had to be performed. My life had shrunk, and when I thought of past events, when I talked to my parents on the phone, when I saw an acquaintance or fellow student on the street, all these things seemed to be from another lifetime. And I didn't feel well. On several occasions I suffered dizzy spells and would sink to my knees in an effort to stay conscious. Their frequency upset me, and I wondered if I hadn't contracted some rare brain disease or

invisible cancer. Sometimes I imagined lumps growing on
my body. Then one evening at work, I fainted, sending a
tray of two chicken curry salads and a glass of Bordeaux
crashing to the floor. When I came to, I was fired. Bob,
the manager, was standing over me, his long face full of
concern. He was sorry, he said, but I was obviously in bad
shape and he was afraid this was the last straw. I was
surprised. "The last straw?" I said. He pushed out his lips
so the top one nearly touched his nose. I couldn't interpret
this facial expression. Then he put his hand on my shoulder
and said in a low, apologetic voice, "There have been complaints." That was August 21, 1979. I had twenty-seven
dollars and change to last me until Columbia started on
September fourth.

My days lost their shape. Order lapsed with the job, and
an hour became impossibly long, a thing to be endured.
I slept a lot and read in bits and pieces, and then with
darkness I continued my roaming, seeking out the same
places I had gone when I was working. But now there was
no money. The bartenders let me drink water out of kindness or offered me a drink on the house. My stomach was
giving me trouble, though, and nothing could soothe it.
Walking made me overly tired and I was unsteady on my
feet. Just a little longer, I said to myself. Hang in there
until you get your stipend check. Then you'll fix everything.
But the university, only blocks away, had become an ab-
straction, and I no longer believed in it. I thought of Philosophy Hall, of my talks with Professor Rose, remembering
his office like the detailed setting in a novel, which I could
imagine perfectly but never really visit. You can't go back
there now, I said. Give it up.

The afternoon before it all blew up in my face, the

telephone rang. The noise stunned me because I was sure the phone was unplugged. I must have forgotten to disconnect it when I called my parents, I thought. I answered it but heard nothing. Then I heard breathing. "Paris," I said. "Is that you? Can you hear me?" There was no answer. I started screaming into the phone. "Leave me alone! This is no time for tricks, whoever you are! Can't you understand that? I'm barely alive, do you hear me? I'm barely alive, so go away!" I heard a click. For a long time I sat on the floor shaking, hearing my own words again with astonishment. Did I really believe that? Maybe I had howled my guts out to some stranger who had dialed the wrong number. I unplugged the phone from the wall. When night came, I put on the suit pants and a T-shirt. I took the suit jacket over my arm. It was too hot to wear outside, but in the air-conditioned bars it was a necessity. I was headed for the Babydoll Lounge, where I hoped to find Ramona. When I arrived, she was there, stripping on the little platform across from the booths. She looked adorable with a ponytail and those glasses, removing her clothes with an ease and generosity I admired. Ramona smiled and waved at the spectators and seemed to enjoy herself, unlike the other stripper, a woman named Billie, who moved in a trance of narcissistic absorption, displaying her tight, athletic body without ever seeing us. Ramona nodded at me when I walked in, and the acknowledgment made me unusually happy. The music was something old and raucous, but it had melody and my spirits rose. I sat down and ordered a brandy, squandering two dollars I might have eaten with, but I threw the bills on the bar plus a tip without even looking at them. I was casual, easy, delighted with myself. Rita, an alcoholic regular who wept in her booze, brushed

past me, and I smiled back at her broadly, genuinely glad
to see her. The brandy lightened my head almost immediately, and I stared at the bottles behind the bar shining
in the mirror. How beautiful they are, I thought. The world
is more beautiful than you remember, and it's cool in here.
The good air, I said to myself, and put on my jacket. A
policeman walked in and sat down beside me. I'd never
seen him before, but Ed, the bartender, seemed to know
him, and the two men instantly launched into a discussion
about the New York Mets. The officer was young and
chubby. The flesh around his middle bulged over his pants,
tightening the blue cloth of his shirt near his gun. I stared
at the weapon protruding beyond the roll of fat. I wondered
if it was heavy. It was so close to me. My knee was within
inches of it. I could have brushed it. Then I let my knee
graze it. The man didn't move. He was deep in conversation. I took another sip of brandy and looked down at
the gun again. It sat firmly in the holster, an inanimate
appendage, so peculiar I wanted to laugh, but it fascinated
me too. What would it be like to hold it? Quickly I let my
gaze move across the room. No one was looking at me.
The urge was powerful. Turning on the barstool, I let my
hand dangle near the gun, my fingers touching its handle.
Still the officer made no sign. Should I take it out slowly,
or pull it from him in one swift motion? I had no plans
for the gun, no wish to fire it, no idea what to do with it
once I had it. What I burned to do was simply take it.
Then I gently wrapped my fingers around the gun and
began to inch it out of the holster. The policeman lurched
backward, clamping down on my wrist with his hand and
swinging himself around suddenly so he faced me. "Crazy
broad! What the fuck are you doing?" he yelled. He yanked

my hand up in the air; his grip hurt. The bar was silent except for the music that continued to blare. Everyone looked at me. I saw Ramona, now still and unsmiling. She moved her lips soundlessly. I think she mouthed "Klaus." Ed was gesturing fast. "What happened?" "She had my gun, for Christ's sake!" I said nothing. There was more chatter, discussion. The policeman leaned over the bar, still holding my wrist away from him, but he loosened his grip on me. I pulled away hard and ran for the door. Someone grabbed my sleeve on the way out, but I ripped it away and went through the door, feeling the hot air come down on me like a weight. There were voices behind me. I heard the door close, then shouts for me to stop. I thought I heard Ramona call for me to come back. I tore down West Broadway to White Street, to Church, and then up to Canal, crossing in traffic and running around the corner at Grand, searching for a place to hide. On Wooster Street I ducked into a doorway. All was quiet. No one had bothered to follow me that far, but I didn't move. Sitting down on the landing, I looked out into the deserted street. Nothing moved. Dead minutes. Then, as if by magic, a breeze blew up in the stillness, scattering some newspapers that sailed onto the sidewalk. I took off my jacket, observing the motion of my fingers as I laid them on my arm. This can't be my hand, I thought, but the long, tiny bones were unmistakable. The familiarity came as a jolt, and then I heard someone call "Iris!" I looked down the street. It was my mother's voice. But she isn't in New York, I said to myself. You're hearing things. My legs were stiff, and one foot hurt. Removing my sneaker, I saw a gash below my right ankle, but I couldn't place the injury. I sat there for a while before I put the shoe back on and headed for the subway. I paid the fare with fifty cents I always carried in my sock and limped home from the 110th Street station.

Once inside my apartment, I walked straight to the long mirror in my bedroom. For weeks I hadn't looked at myself, had always avoided it in fact, but I took a good hard look at the dirty, skeletal person with the shorn head and baggy pants cinched at the waist by a ragged belt, a person with no breasts to speak of. They had disappeared with the pounds, but the emaciation wasn't what scared me. In my face I saw a morbid change. My eyes were different. They seemed to have gone quiet. I remember that I wanted to sob but I couldn't. Then I took off my pants and folded them very carefully, which made no sense because they were filthy, as was the jacket which I also smoothed out and put away with the trousers in a plastic bag deep in my closet. For at least an hour I sat in the bathtub and cleaned my body. I was meticulous, energetic. Then sitting naked on a chair, I telephoned my parents and in an astonishingly calm voice explained that I needed money for the week. I had lost my job and couldn't get by any longer. Not a lot, I said, just a little. My father wired more than I had asked for, two hundred and fifty dollars. It was manna from the sky. With it, I ate, a bit more every day so as not to shock my system. I bought expensive vegetables and meats, preparing three meals a day, chewing every bite methodically, waiting to see how my stomach would respond. It did well. Food was my salvation, and I imagined that I was getting fatter, that the roundness was returning to my body at an impossible rate. With every mouthful, I was burying Klaus, piling more and more dirt on top of him to keep him down. I worked at my own recovery like a robot programmed for survival, determined to come back to myself. The idea was to arrive at registration on the fourth fattened and blooming. The day came, and I went in a new dress ($39.99 on sale), thinking myself quite restored, even lovely, but my old acquaintances greeted me with shocked looks and exclamations about my weight and hair. Yes, yes, I said, I'd been sick, but I was much better now, a long bout of flu, quite severe. My hair had fallen out in big clumps so I cut it. It's growing in, though. I'm sure I was ludicrous, a dolled-up corpse, half crazed with hope for a second chance. Then out of the corner of my eye I saw him, a slender, handsome boy with a serious expression. In his hand was a copy of *The Portable Nietzsche*.

The boy was Stephen. He didn't speak to me then, but a month later, we became lovers, of a kind. I chased him for eight months, and he was hot and cold for the duration, never sure whether he wanted me or not. I didn't tell him about Klaus. Several times the desire to confess the whole story came to my throat and mouth, but it never passed into words. Ruth called me a few times, and we had a couple of dinners together. I drycleaned the suit but didn't return it. It hung in my closet in its transparent bag. Paris telephoned as soon as I plugged in the machine on September fourth. "Jesus Christ," he said. "I've been calling for weeks. You went underground, you devil. I thught you might be dead, lying on the street somewhere with no ID, already buried in Potter's Field. I even went to your goddamn building and buzzed you. Nobody home. Nobody home." "I'm sorry," I said. "It was a bad time. I can't talk about it." And we didn't. Now I marvel at our silence, but to have told it then would have been impossible, and the fact that Paris knew but didn't ask seemed a testament to his loyalty. Still his knowledge of Klaus was there, unspo-

ken but absolute, a paradoxical thing, because it brought
both unnatural intimacy and suspicion. He called. We had
lunch together. Paris was often away from the city, however. He had many fish to fry, and I saw him infrequently.
In those days I stuck close to the university, feeling safer
there than in the wilds of downtown. But by May Stephen
was gone, and I faced another summer alone in the city.
Vowing never to waitress again, I took odd jobs of an
academic sort, doing research for a medical historian, an
old man who regarded me with a mixture of contempt and
lust. The lost twenty pounds were back, and my hair had
grown to chin length. In the streets men craned their heads
to look, and in grocery stores, at bus stops, any place where
I wasn't moving, they addressed me with hope in their
eyes. I took up smoking for a while, Marlboros in the red
box. Cigarettes seemed to steady me then, but I had to
give them up when I got sick. In July Mr. Morning came
along, for whom I wrote reports, another story altogether,
but by the time I left him, I was desperate for money again,
and the headaches started, bad ones that struck like lightning and left me wretched and depressed.

In August I got work as an English instructor for low-
level employees in an insurance company. My seven students were eager to better themselves, and one young man
named Jefferson had the sharpest memory I've encoun-
tered. He never forgot a word I said. We met every day
for four weeks, and one day near the end, I was looking
at Jefferson and he was looking at me, and half his face
vanished. It didn't last long, but I stopped talking and
clutched my chair. That hole wasn't the first and it wouldn't
be the last, but staring into the black emptiness, I believed
it was real. I thought a part of his face was gone. Only

later was I able to tell myself that I had suffered a migraine aura. The following months were a time when the everyday became precarious. At any moment an ordinary thing, a table or chair, a face or hand, might disappear, and with the blindness came a feeling that I was no longer whole. I had put myself back together and now my body was failing me. I knew the damned thing would crack.

That fall I studied hard for my oral exams in the spring. I read the plays, poems, novels, and essays on the fantastically long list and then forgot them. My brain was a sieve. The words were wrapped in gauze, one letter as blurred as the next. The pain in my head was sometimes weak, sometimes strong, but it rarely left me. At Christmastime I went home to Webster and was well for two weeks, but in January I finally went to pieces. By then I had seen several neurologists with no luck. It was Dr. Fish who put me in the hospital. He gave me giant pills of Thorazine, a drug that made me so inert I couldn't wiggle my toes. My thoughts, however, were a madhouse of insight and delusion, and I hadn't the least idea which was which. After ten days, I checked myself out. Dr. Fish, whom I had hardly seen, was annoyed, but I pulled my frail carcass out of the bed, dressed, and tottered out to the desk in the hospital lobby. "I'm signing out," I told the woman there. After I gave her my name, she presented me with a bill for $2,038.46 and asked me to pay it before I left. My university insurance had covered eighty percent of the bill. This was the remaining sum. I stared into her brown eyes and examined her straightened hair, combed smoothly behind her ears. The pain in my head seemed to put her at a great distance but at the same time, she was paradoxically large, like a person on a movie screen.

She was speaking to me, explaining hospital procedure, telling me what had to be done. The bill was in my hand, and I studied the numbers. Stupidly I began to ponder the forty-six cents. I can pay that, I thought. Yes, that can easily be paid. The change was in my pocket. "Are you all right?" said the woman. I looked at her. She was lovely. Her skin was nearly black. I stared at it, then gazed down at the bill. "I'm sick," I said to her finally, explaining myself to her simply. She gave me a perplexed look and waved someone over to the desk, a man. "Talk to her," she said. "She doesn't seem to understand about the bill." The man was large and white, with pink blotches on his cheeks and forehead. I heard his voice drone on about what was expected, but rather than meet his eyes, I brought the paper very close to my face and read the numbers again. "Young lady," he was saying. I'm unwell, I said to myself, sick as a dog. "The money . . . " he said. "Do you need time . . . " Slowly, thoughtfully, I folded the bill into a tiny square, put the paper in my mouth, and ate it. Walking across the lobby, I listened to their voices rise in protest, and when I put my hand on the door, the man said, "Let her go. We'll bill her through the mail. She's obviously got a screw loose."

I walked home through the park in the snow. As soon as I was inside my apartment, I fell into bed. Just before I slept, I thought to myself, He's back, but it doesn't matter. Nothing matters anymore. I slept for two days, waking intermittently to the pain and then falling again into unconsciousness. When I finally woke up, it was nighttime, and it seemed to me that the migraine was thinner, less severe. A tremendous excitement at the prospect of being well came over me. I sat trembling on the edge of the bed

and caught a glimpse of myself in the mirror. You've lost
weight again, I thought. You must eat. But I wasn't hungry.
I went to the closet, unwrapped the suit, and put it on.
It's all right, I told myself. There's nothing to be done about
it now. You can't go on the way you've been going. It was
Klaus who ate the bill, after all, and silly as it was, there's
a lot to be said for it. I went out the door, but this time I
headed north toward Harlem, and when I crossed the
threshold at 125th Street, I knew it was beginning again.

Because I had no classes to attend, just exams to prepare,
I was free to hide. I took out my phone again, using it
only to call my parents once every two weeks. The truth
is, I didn't want anyone to see me sick. Although the
migraines were better, I still had bad fits of nausea and
vomiting, bowel trouble and periods of stupefying exhaustion. No doctor could help me. I had to handle it
myself, and I discovered that if I lay in bed and chanted,
repeating over and over the little incantation "Never mind,"
I could dampen the pain considerably. I chanted a lot in
those days. When I looked at the list of books I was supposed to know and felt the panic rise in my chest, I chanted.
Each time the hospital sent a bill, I chanted. After an aura,
I chanted. Before a meal, I chanted to keep the food down.
And Klaus? I needed Klaus, and despite my sense that I
had fallen again, the walks at night did me good, cleared
my head. I haunted the Upper West Side, sporting the suit
under the winter coat I had bought at a secondhand store—
a man's greatcoat. And I had my hair cut so short that
when I touched my neck, I felt bristle. I avoided the bars
frequented by students and stuck to the seedier neighborhood joints. Again I found people unruffled by my eccentricity. The nights were dangerous. I walked where I

shouldn't have walked alone, but my recklessness pleased me. I sang loudly in the darkness, whistled at strangers, and once, I wrote NEVER MIND in huge letters on a wall with spray paint I had bought specifically for that purpose. These misdemeanors left me both invigorated and guilty. Each night, I told myself it was the last. Then in one of my late spots, a place called Stars, I bumped into Professor Rose.

The bartender at Stars was an obese man who went by the name Toots. He was a sweaty, kind man who worried or pretended to worry about me. He had already been fed the pack of lies about Klaus or Klausina and had listened with sympathy. At the same time, it wasn't clear to me that he believed these stories. He winked at me often and had a very intelligent look about him.

"Klaus," he said to me one night. "It's time you got some new clothes. You're a good-looking girl, you know, and that shabby suit looks dumb. Dumb, girl. Do you hear me? I don't want to interfere, mind you. I'm not the interfering kind. It's none of my business, but I say it's a shame, and what's more, I know you're not a dyke. There's not a dyke in the world as sweet as you."

"Thanks, Toots," I said. "I guess you mean that as a compliment." I looked down at my brandy.

"And you've got to put some meat on those bones, fill out. Why, a strong wind would blow you away."

"Yes, Toots," I said, and smiled at him.

"Let me get you a burger from the kitchen," he said. "It's on the house."

"That's okay," I said. "Don't bother with it."

Toots feigned deafness and went into the ktichen. The

bar wasn't crowded. It was late. A headache had set in, but it was mild. I realized I wanted the hamburger and was glad. Toots waddled back with a plate, fussing with the napkin and silverware. "Eat up, honey," he said, and I felt a hand on my shoulder. It was Professor Rose. He studied me.

"Iris?" he said. "Is it you?"

"Yes," I whispered.

Toots was leaning on the bar. "Everything okay, Klaus?" Professor Rose gave him a sharp look.

"Yes," I said.

"Come with me," said my teacher, and taking my hamburger in one hand and my elbow with the other, he led me to a booth and gently pressed me into the seat. He sat down across from me and folded his arms. His face was the same, and the familiarity aroused me. I looked at the wall and felt his eyes. When I turned, his expression was ironic, the wary beginning of a smile on his lips. "What are you doing here? What's happened to you?"

I blushed. "I've been sick," I said. "I know I look terrible."

He leaned back and shook his head.

"I might ask you the same question," I said. "An eminent professor like yourself. What are you doing here? This is a dump, in case you hadn't noticed."

He grinned. "Even eminent professors need to get out of their apartments and have a drink late at night every once in a while. I live a block from here, Iris."

I watched him hesitate. He had heard Toots call me Klaus, and I guessed he was searching for the right words. He waved his left hand just above the table's surface, and I remembered the mannerism. "Iris," he said. "You're in

some kind of trouble. Maybe I can help you." He paused.
"I often thought of sending you a note from North Carolina,
but it never got done."

I'm not sure whether it was the unwritten letter or just
his voice that undid me, but I felt my face contort and my
mouth quiver. One or the other was the catalyst for what
must have been months of pent-up self-pity. In good times
I cry often, shedding tears easily, but when times are bad,
my ducts go dry and I almost never weep. The misery I
felt then was grief. I wanted her back, my old self, the girl
who had watched him go, and she was dead. I had mucked
it up. Stephen, the hospital, my meager bank account, the
suit, the half-eaten hamburger on my plate, all seemed
equally pitiful, equally to blame, and I wept my heart out.
I shook and sobbed and made a scene. The good, nosy
Toots whisked my plate away and looked suspiciously at
Professor Rose. "Klausey, Klausey," he said, patting my
arm. "It can't be as bad as all that. You want me to get rid
of this character?"

"It's not him, Toots." I honked into the paper napkin.
"It's me."

"I'll take care of her," said Professor Rose. He paid the
bill and helped me out of the booth.

"We'll go to my office," he said, once we were in the
street. "It's quiet there, and we can talk."

I nodded. We walked the four blocks in silence and
turned into the university gate, moving quickly toward
Philosophy Hall. He unlocked the door and we took the
stairs to the sixth floor. I said nothing while he put the
key in his office door, opened it, and made a gesture for
me to sit down. He pulled his chair close to mine and put

his hands on his knees. His face was the image of paternal concern. He's going to berate me, I thought.

He wrinkled his forehead. "Klaus? That man called you Klaus."

"I use the name sometimes," I said. "It's kind of a game with me."

"A game! What kind of game?"

"Does it matter to you?" An involuntary gasp escaped me. I was still recovering from my crying jag.

"Yes, it matters. I care about you. I walk into a bar at midnight and stumble onto one of my best students downing brandy and looking like something out of Dickens, for God's sake. Those clothes and hair and that awful man calling you Klaus? What am I supposed to think?"

"He's not an awful man."

"All right," he said, turning toward the blackened window. "He's not awful."

I stared at his profile. He had a good nose. "I missed you," I said. "I know now that I missed you terribly." The ease with which I said these words surprised me.

He turned to me, his expression sad. He let his arms fall to his sides. "Iris, you disarm me. I don't know what to say."

We looked at each other for a long time, and he made no effort to disguise the torment in his face. Then, like a defeated man, he sighed. I saw his shoulders sink, and he reached out for me. He took me by the forearms and pulled me into him.

We were noisy lovers that night in Philosophy Hall. I'm sure we made a racket, falling to the floor in a desperate heap under the harsh fluorescent light, and I know I screamed in crisis and that he talked to me, but I can't remember what he said, probably what everybody says, the name of the other person or just "yes"—words fraught with meaning only when they are spoken. To repeat them is sacrilege. In short, we ate each other alive, and when it was over, we lay in silence, stunned, I think, by what had happened.

The room was cold. I shivered and he held me. The suit lay crumpled beside us, and despite the chill, I was reluctant to put it on. Professor Rose covered me with his jacket, and after a time, he said, "I don't think you should do it anymore."

"What?"

"Klaus."

I welcomed the sanction, knew I had been waiting for it, had hoped for it. "I know," I said. "I won't."

I started calling him Michael. In the beginning when I used the name, I always experienced a rush of feeling, a strong sense of having moved into a new position: universities may be the last place in America where first names still have the force of intimacy. "Michael" was for me a clandestine sign, a key to our secret, and I used the name over and over, to him and to myself. We saw each other late in the afternoon, when my window briefly caught the sunlight and then lost it. The light was important because even when he wasn't there with me, the sun's four o'clock slant was rife with erotic associations. He was an intense lover, and his zeal created in me a new sense of my own otherness. Sometimes after he was gone, I would examine myself naked in the mirror, and for an instant would imagine I saw what he saw—an enchanted body. Michael Rose wasn't beautiful. He had a large, ragged appendix scar, a little extra flesh around his middle, and his blue veins were clearly visible through the pale skin of his legs. There were moments when the physical fact of the man estranged me, when my idea of the man and the man himself were disconnected, but they lasted only seconds. I was seduced through my ear. The more he talked, the more I wanted him, and he talked up a storm, wooing me with Catullus, Boccaccio, Donne, and Sidney, with Shakespeare and Wyatt, Fielding and Joyce, and that's how I like to remember him now, in midsentence, lying in my bed with his eyes shut, quoting from memory.

He didn't tell me very much about himself, however. I knew that he had a wife and three older children, and that he had lived "almost" his whole life in New York City. Both his parents were dead. In the beginning I pressed him for details, but his reluctance made me stop. Once when I asked him to tell me about his boyhood, he said, "My father beat me, and when I was ten, I ran away with a band of Gypsies."

"No," I said. "The real story."

"My father beat me, and I spent my childhood waiting for the Gypsies."

"Is that true?"

"More or less."

"How much more or less?"

He smiled with one side of his mouth. "Oh, I don't know. It's not that I don't remember, I do. Sometimes I find it odd that I'm not a kid anymore, that I'm getting old. I wonder where my baseball glove is. Whatever happened to Charlie Shapiro?"

"Why don't you tell me about all of that?"

"I'll tell you, Iris, one day, but this isn't the time to dredge it up. Telling all is a dubious form of generosity. Some things are better not told."

And that was all. He left me with a bad father, the Gypsies, and Charlie Shapiro.

We didn't talk about Klaus. I wanted to tell him, but the words that might have announced my feelings about those nights were buried, and to carry them from that hidden place to my mouth required an effort I couldn't make. Michael was too close to the origins of my wanderings, was a collaborator of sorts, and I had a strong instinct to keep him out of it, even though I knew it was Michael who killed Klaus. After that night in Philosophy Hall, I had lost all desire for the roaming boy. Michael had made him vanish, and I was possessed by the crazy idea that if he could do this, he could also bring Klaus back. Krüger's boy was our Frankenstein's monster, a creation we chose to ignore.

We went on into the spring, and I was well. From time to time, I would fall into bed and chant when my head fogged with an oncoming migraine, but the pain was negligible. The nausea and vomiting were over. I saw no black holes. My hair grew. In March I took my oral exams. For the first hour I spewed out information like an automaton gone berserk, citing names, dates, places, and every scrap of knowledge that appeared in my head. I brought in philosophers, linguists, spun theories and quoted from the novels I loved. Then I ran out of gas, puffing and sputtering my way through the last hour and my three minor fields, forgetting what I thought I knew, and I saw the faces of the five middle-aged men on my committee, amused only minutes before, drop into identical expressions of pity and concern. They passed me anyway. I knew so much and so little. That was that. They were kind. I was humbled. Michael said, "It's a rite of passage, nothing more. Put it behind you." But I replayed my stumped moments over and over, stung by regret, and I thought, If only I had stayed at home reading the Metaphysical poets instead of running around the city like some half-cocked drifter.

Not long after that, Michael spent the night with me. His wife was out of town. We had never had so many hours together, and by morning we were changed. The difference was subtle, but it hinged yet again on the story. Michael told me that Columbia University Press would publish the novella. He had written a preface, and I would get full credit for the translation.

"You don't seem exactly overjoyed," he said.

I looked at him. "But your name has to be on the translation," I said.

"It's yours. You did all the hard work."

"That's not true. It's just as much yours as it is mine!"

He sat up in bed and adjusted the pillow behind him. "What are we talking about here, Iris?"

"You know. You've always known. I can't stand the pretense. I really can't."

He put his hands up and started waving them.

"Don't do that," I said.

He stopped and turned to me. "Iris, I can't read your mind."

I crossed my legs Indian style and looked at him. "You said a long time ago that it was a Pandora's box."

"I was talking about our working together."

"No you weren't."

"Iris," he said, a sad lilt in his voice.

"There's something about the story, something in it that was horribly exciting, and it got to us."

"Iris." His voice was soft. "You're the one who borrowed the name. To what end, I've never properly understood. I haven't wanted to pry. But that's why you're upset now. Fiction is not life."

"You don't believe that."

"I think I do."

"You know as well as I do that the line can't be drawn, that we're infected at every moment by fictions of all kinds, that it's inescapable."

"Don't be a sophist," he said. "There is a world and it's palpable."

"I don't mean that," I said. "I mean that it's hard really to see it, that it's all hazy with our dreams and fantasies."

"You're talking about Klaus, your Klaus."

"Our Klaus," I said. "Do you know that for one moment I thought you had written the damned story."

He grinned. "I wish I had."

"You see," I said. "You adopted it, took it on, and the thing is, it's cruel."

"There are lots of cruel stories, both real and imagined."

"Yes, but—"

"But this one got under your skin."

"Our skin," I said.

"We're not one and the same, Iris."

"I know, but I can feel that it's between us—no, of us. There's a piece of the puzzle you've never shown me."

"You're being mysterious."

"And you're hiding."

He sighed. Then he reached over and touched my hair.

"I know it sounds demented," I said. "But that missing part, that thing between us, I think it's evil."

"Evil?" His eyes clouded, and he pressed his lips together until they turned white. "What is evil?"

"I don't know."

"Is Klaus evil?" he said quickly, his eyes narrowed. He looked straight at me.

"He doesn't kill the cat."

"No, but he meant to," he said. "Is he evil? Is it a peccadillo, or a crime?"

"The law has its measurements," I said.

"Yes," he said, "but we all imagine committing crimes, and there's no penalty for fantasy. Klaus is full of nasty ideas. What if he had never acted out any of them? Does that make him less evil? Surely evil consists of more than the bad act."

"I didn't say he was evil."

"So the person and the act can be separated, is that right?"

"I'm not sure."

"The law has endless allowances, doesn't it? Temporary insanity, hormonal swings—too much testosterone, menopausal manias, postpartum depressions, too much junk food—drove him to murder. It's the the-devil-made-me-do-it theory of defense. But aren't we the demons?"

"Yes," I whispered to him. "We are."

He said nothing.

"But to think something terrible is not the same as doing it." I shuddered as I spoke. "When do people turn their thoughts into action?" I felt cold and put the blanket over my legs. I saw the policeman's gun, and seeing it in my mind made me want to scream. I clamped my jaw shut and closed my eyes.

"A barrier is lifted. In some people it's never formed. For others it means crashing down the gate. And then I think sometimes you just open the door and walk through—like nothing. Unspeakable crimes have been made routine, orderly." He paused and took a breath, looking away from me at the wall. "Every day, people do the incredible. I don't just mean political torture far away. I know a woman who threw her three-year-old son out the window. She jumped out after him, but she didn't die. She's still alive."

"Did you know her well?"

"For a time I did. I visited her in the hospital. Lila knew her best. They were very close, but Lila was so angry she couldn't see her . . ."

A chill took my entire body, and my teeth chattered. "That woman, she must have been out of her mind."

"Yes, I suppose, but what does that mean? We're back to the same place. Where do you locate responsibility?"

I studied the spines on my books that lined the wall. "I've often felt that ideas of goodness, of the truth, have to be unbending, absolute, or everything falls apart."

He looked at me. "You mustn't confuse virtue and the truth. The two are very different."

The words took hold, and my mistake jarred me.

"Virtue is a moral quality distinct from what's true," he said.

I nodded. "So that evil can be the truth."

"Of course."

"But none of this explains what it is."

Michael shook his head.

"Do you think Augustine was right?" I said. "I mean, that evil is a kind of lapse or distance, a falling away?"

"He was avoiding dualism, Iris. The whole argument is predicated on a belief in God . . ."

"I know, but he must have felt it that way, that evil was an emptiness, a lack of something, not a presence."

He turned his head fast and looked at me. "That's what desire is, isn't it? The lack of something." He sounded angry. Then he grabbed my upper arms with his hands and shook me, not hard but firmly. "You want to hear the truth?" he said. "Goodness aside. I'm going to make you run. You're going to hate me before we're through. I feel it, that pit, that emptiness. I'm going to lose you." He laughed for an instant and dropped his hands. "The terrible irony is that more than anything in the world I want you to stay."

His speech was like a crack in the world. When he spoke, it was true, and I felt I had seen not only into him but into other people, into myself. But then I shook it off. It was melodrama. We were carried away. "Don't say that," I said. "You can't predict the future . . ."

"We've talked too much," he said. "It's late. We're here together now." He embraced me tightly, crushing my face against his chest. I had to pull my head away to breathe.

During the night, he slept badly, shifting his position often and mumbling to himself. He woke me near morning when he cried out in his sleep, but then he grew quiet. I didn't catch the words. It's guilt, I thought. I imagined his wife, whom I had never seen—a slender, aging woman with a soft face and long brown hair tied up at the neck. God only knows where this image came from—it must

have been a collage of the long line of faculty wives I had
known in my life—but that is how I saw her, and the sight
made me pity her, and him, and I thought to myself, I've
betrayed someone I don't even know. I spoke her name
inwardly. Lila, I said. It's a pretty name.

At breakfast Michael was jittery, distracted. His eyes were
red, and he rubbed them often. I half expected him to leap
up from the table and run to the door.

"My God," I said. "You'd think the secret police were
coming for you. Relax."

He was embarrassed. "Sorry."

I smiled at him. "You've never seen me in the morning
before. I'm probably scaring you away. I bet I look like a
witch." I made a face at him, pulling my mouth to either
side with my fingers and bulging my eyes.

He laughed. "You're a witch, all right," he said, reaching
across the table to pat my head. "But you're beautiful."

Within minutes of that comment, he was gone. His absence produced a new feeling in me, a mixture of dread
and guilt. I washed the dishes very slowly, scrubbing each
one methodically, holding it up to the window light to
make sure it shone. Then I cleaned the entire apartment.

That same week, Paris called and invited me to see a movie
at the Thalia. Michael was with me in the afternoon. At
six he was still there. I told him I had to get dressed to go
to the movies. While I was putting on my lipstick, Michael
stood behind me in the bathroom.

"Who's taking you to the movies?"

"No one's *taking* me. I'm meeting a friend."

"What friend?"

"Paris. I've told you about Paris."

"The art critic?"

"Yes, Michael, the small, unattractive, but not uninteresting art critic."

Michael looked pained. He put on his jacket. "I'd better leave now," he said. "So you can get ready."

"Wait a minute," I said. "You're married. You go home every night to her." It was a television conversation. I knew it, but I continued. "Do you want me to stay here and mope?"

"I didn't say that," he said. "I know very well that I'm not in a position to say anything."

The little miseries started then. All the way to the Thalia, I went over the scene, rethinking my language. I wished I had stated my case better. When I saw Paris, I hugged him for the first time.

"What was that for?"

"I've missed you." I smiled into his face. Paris took my arm and we walked into the dark theater. It was not crowded, and I let my legs hang over the seat in front of me. Someone several rows in front of us farted loudly. Paris and I exchanged smiles. The film was *Sunrise*, directed by F. W. Murnau in 1927. I can't remember its sequence well, and I can't reconstruct the whole story, but I remember its effect on me, and the way the city looked in the movie—a carnival in hell, a grotesque playground; and I believed it. Paris turned to look at me every once in a while, which made me suspect he was monitoring my responses. The obscure light in the room was amiable, and I felt glad to see no one except the people on the screen, to have Paris next to me without being forced to look at him. After the movie, Paris took me to dinner at the Cafe Luxembourg,

a noisy, fashionable place on the West Side. I gabbed uncontrollably as I let my eyes wander to other tables. The
conversation is lost. I recall only the way it ended. I had
been laughing at some remark Paris had made, when I
noticed he was studying me, his face suddenly serious.
Before he spoke, he put a finger to his pale pink tie, leaned
over and touched a lock of my hair, and then sat back in
his chair.

"Your hair," he said. "It's getting long."

I looked straight at him. "I like it this way."

Paris nodded. "It's pretty," he said. "But it lacks the
audacity of a crew cut, doesn't it?"

I stared at the table. "Yes," I said. "It does."

Michael came and went, but I sensed a difference. In the
early weeks he had luxuriated in our adultery, had come
smiling to my door, but there were times now when he
arrived haggard and serious, like a man on a mission.
Sometimes he would glance at objects in my apartment in
a way that made me think he was looking for something.
His distraction unnerved me. When I asked him about his
mood, he was vague. "Maybe it's too much for you," I said
to him once. "Sneaking in and out of here like a thief." He
just shook his head, and I didn't press him further. The
silence between us had become insinuation, and I didn't
know how to fight it, but at those moments I would see
him from a distance, like a strange man in a crowd. One
afternoon in April, Michael had taken a shower and was
standing near the kitchenette in the outer room of my
apartment. He was wearing only a towel. I put my arms
around his waist and leaned against him.

"Do you always use two coffee cups?" he said, staring into the sink.

"Sometimes I'm too lazy to wash them."

"You weren't entertaining someone?" he said, his voice dull.

I released him and took his shoulders, turning him toward me. "No," I said. "Don't do this. Please. It will hurt us."

He looked at me, nodded, and smiled with his mouth closed. "I know," he said.

But Michael imagined signs of betrayal everywhere: a shirt of Stephen's in my closet I had never returned, flowers Ruth sent me on my birthday, even a letter from my mother lying out on my desk that began, "My darling Iris." He never accused me of anything. His interrogations were circuitous: "You've received flowers?" or "A letter from someone?" Jealousy is rarely unfounded. Although I had no other lovers, Michael had glimpsed my alienation, however momentary, and needed someone to blame. His suspicion brought with it an atmosphere of threat. He would rub his hands hard when he spoke to me, making me think he didn't trust them. At times Michael's jealousy turned me into an awed spectator. At other times it entered me like a sickness, and I would yell in frustration. That was the problem. I was a player and not a player. I was in and out. I became what is known as an impossible woman, one of those horrible creatures who can't make up their minds. But my moods weren't calculated. Michael changed. He was one and then another. He was near and then far. I shuttled back and forth between the two poles and felt the strain.

With Stephen, I had known jealousy from the other side,

had come down with the disease myself, and perhaps that's why the experience was familiar. And yet it was more than that. The ritual of his veiled accusations, my denials, and our eventual reconciliations had the force of reenactment from the first. Whether I was screaming profanity or cooing reassurance, the words I spoke seemed to come from a script as old as the hills, and I felt like a character in a farce. I've come to believe that there is no genuine language of love, only sounds. When I opened my mouth to speak to him, to pour out my pity and affection, it was nonsense to my ears. But we talked on, digging a rut with every sentence. We feasted on the rubbish heap of dead expressions, and the gorging made us worse. He turned pompous or maudlin, I nasty or inane. And so we teetered from one extreme to another, truly present in neither. Then we would find ourselves again and speak to each other in the old way, and there were hours of happiness. Still, a third presence, invisible and cloying, remained. I began to sense that when he spoke to me, whether it was about literature, philosophy, or science, he was circling around this other thing, this third presence. All his discussions were rife with innuendo. His speech had become less direct, more oblique and delicate. He talked a lot about cruelty, about the mystery of cruelty and the human impulse to maim and destroy. He talked about private sadism and mass barbarism, about psychopaths and the Nazis. There is no end to such discussions. They wind in on themselves. Explanations are spun out and then end in disbelief. Michael was looking for the heart of it, but it couldn't be found, and I knew it was personal and that he was taking me with him, letting me in. He forced my complicity, saying, "You understand," or, "We think alike." But half the time he lost me, and

once when he told me a story about a man who had
survived Auschwitz as a musician and then many years
later committed suicide after he slapped his daughter in
public, I burst into tears. He brought up *The Brutal Boy*
again, studying me when he spoke about Klaus and Krüger's fate in the death camp. "Let's not talk about it anymore," I said. "It gets worse and worse somehow. I wish
I'd never laid eyes on the stupid book." I remember his
exact words then. "We can't turn back the clock now. It's
in us. If we close our eyes, it will jump out at us in the
darkness." I didn't know what the "it" referred to, whether
he meant the story or evil or an amorphous presence, and
I didn't ask. By then I didn't want to hear. At the same
time, I was ensnared like a person in a horror movie who
covers his eyes and then peeks.

Michael's rambling lectures always brought me back to
the bar and to the gun, to what I couldn't tell him. The
episode returned with nauseating repetition. And yet it was
a false memory, because I fled my body and saw myself
do it. In effect, I became a spectator of my own act, one
of the shocked onlookers in the Babydoll Lounge. But it
was you, I said to myself, you who wanted the gun, you
who tried to take it. My motive was inexplicable. The
impulse that had pushed me so far was buried with Klaus.

He brought me gifts, little presents of food and books
but also things: a bottle of perfume, tiny earrings of topaz
and gold, and a crystal vase for the flowers I had been
keeping in an old mayonnaise jar. I loved these offerings
and loved his face when I opened the boxes. He looked
young then and eager to please. But these tokens also made
my life less stark. Owning them pulled me farther away
from the bleakness of having nothing. They were symbolic,

of course, but when I looked at the vase filled with tulips, daisies, anemones, or freesia, I was comforted. In early June Michael gave me what would be my last present from him. He had taken me out to dinner at a small French restaurant not far from my apartment but outside the Columbia orbit. It was a risk and we took it. We were celebrating my summer job. I was to teach freshman English at Queens College, and the salary, small as it was, promised to keep me solvent. We ate and drank and laughed. Several times he reached across the table and squeezed my hand. The next day he would leave for the summer. His wife owned a house in Vermont, and he would join her there for July and August. The subject of our parting was taboo, and we didn't mention it. Michael worried about leaving me in the city alone, and I knew he was tormented by fantasies of me with other men. I read it in his eyes and mouth, in his body, and in his oblique but ominous references to "the summer."

After dinner, he handed me a box. The paper was gold and it was tied with a pale blue ribbon. I opened it slowly, pulled aside the tissue, and found a silk scarf—white, navy, red, and green. It was beautiful and expensive, with the name of the designer written in one corner. I held it up. "I've never had anything like this," I said, and draped it over my shoulders. I leaned forward and kissed him. By the time we left, it was almost eleven-thirty, and we began the walk back to my apartment. Michael put his arm around my shoulder and hugged me close to him. We could have met any number of people we knew, but he was throwing caution to the wind, and it made me happy.

"These familiar streets," he said. "I've been here too long."

"How long?"

"Almost fifteen years."

We said nothing, and then I spoke. "I've been here three years now. I've walked these streets hundreds of times. The rhythm is in my feet." I nodded ahead of me. "I bet I could walk this last stretch blindfolded."

I felt his fingers dig into my arm, and he turned his face sharply toward me. Then he moved his hand to my neck and caressed the scarf, rubbing his third finger into my skin. "You're on," he said. "Let's see if you can do it."

"You're kidding."

One side of his mouth twitched, and even in the dark I caught the green of his eyes. He stopped and untied the scarf. "Turn around," he said.

His words brought a tremor of excitement that I felt in my abdomen and an involuntary tightening in my stomach and thighs. He was methodically folding the scarf on his lifted knee and wobbled for a second on one leg. "Turn around," he repeated.

I did, and he pulled the silk scarf around my eyes, knotting it tightly at the back of my head.

"This is crazy, you know," I said.

I saw nothing. The material was dense. "I'm really blind," I said.

"Can you get home?"

"Yes," I said. "We're at a Hundred and Third. I can count the blocks. But you have to keep me from walking into buildings or cars."

"Of course." He laughed.

"Are people looking at us?" I said.

He had a hand on my elbow. "Do you care?" he said.

"No. Let's start."

He removed his hand. I walked slowly forward, feeling for the curb with every step, determined not to fall.

"You're weaving," he said.

"Even blind people have canes, for God's sake."

There was a breeze. I remember wondering if there were stars, wishing I had looked, for some reason. Michael was close to me. I went over the curb awkwardly, feeling exposed in the night air. I laughed. "Is everyone staring?" I said.

"The whole world is staring," he said. "They think we're mad."

But there weren't many people on the street at that hour. I heard footsteps coming toward us, and I stopped. Michael spoke in a low, clear voice but not to me. "It's a wager, madam, a simple wager."

The steps quickened. I burst out laughing. My shoulders shook. Michael laughed too, pulling me toward him and kissing my cheeks and chin. "Time out," he said.

Those six blocks were an odyssey. My equilibrium was gone with my sight, and I lurched and tottered forward, marking each block in my head. Once, Michael reached out to guide me, but I pushed him away, saying, "I can do it."

At 109th Street I turned, holding my hands in front of me. Michael never left my side, and his presence in the blackness was an advantage. His body, although invisible, occupied a certain place, and I heard him breathe and cough, listened for his voice, and imagined his wry face. Groping, I discovered the brick wall of my building and let one hand graze it, expecting the stoop at any moment, but I miscalculated and hit a metal object, stumbling to one side. Michael grabbed me around the waist, and I slumped into him, exhausted. "It's a garbage can," he said. "But you've done it."

I reached for the scarf to pull it off, but he took my hand. "Not yet," he said.

"But I'm too tired. I can't do it anymore."

"I'll take you," he said. "Keep it on until we're inside."

Michael picked me up off my feet and carried me up the steps. His strength seemed remarkable, and I gave way to it, letting my cheek rest against him. The last person who carried me like this, I thought, was my father when he lifted me out of the car where I had been sleeping. It was years and years ago. Michael dropped me to my feet and took my bag. I heard the jingle of keys, the sound of the door. He pulled me inside. The light in the hallway shone through the cloth over my eyes. Again he carried me. "You'll hurt yourself, Michael," I said.

But he didn't answer. He breathed heavily up the single small flight of stairs, again let me stand while he opened the door and drew me inside. I heard the door slam. I think he kicked it with his foot. Again I went for the scarf and again he stopped me, saying, "No, not now. I want you blind, just this once."

He kissed me, and it was good not to see him. He could have been any man. The anonymity was his and mine. Like a child, I felt that my blindness made me disappear, or at least made the boundaries of my body unstable. One of us gasped. I didn't know who it was, and this confusion made my heart pound.

We were in the other room. He had his hands on my shoulders and pressed me down on the bed. There was no light. He was fast, tugging at my clothes. Blind, I thought, the word stirring me. I'm going under. He had taken my wrists and held them above me in a gesture of conquest, and the recognition aroused me. I took the role and played it. The pleasure was in the staging, the idea of ourselves as a repetition of others. I knew this without saying it, felt my femininity as the game of all women, a mysterious identification in which I lost myself. He was caught too, and I wondered what he saw, whom he saw. It didn't matter. Let's drown, I thought, and I felt my pulse in my temples beneath the tight cloth. But then he seemed to race past me, to be overtaken by urgency. I moved my face close to his to kiss him, but he turned away. I searched for a new rhythm, but there was none. The blanket underneath me irritated the skin of my back. I wanted to tug at the blindfold, to adjust it, but he held my arms, intent, feverish. His skin was hot and clammy. I wandered from the drama in my mind, and my body went dead. His hands hurt my wrists, and I struggled to free them, but he jerked me back onto the warm sheet and his fury shocked me. It's strange that one thinks at such moments, that thoughts move freely, that I remembered our conversations. Unspeakable acts, seizures of cruelty, Klaus. I choked on my fear, heard a noise come from me, an animal sound of alarm, and then I said, "No!" He put his hand over my mouth. "Shhhh! Someone will hear you." "No!" I cried out again, fighting him with my free hand. He grabbed it, but I kicked underneath him and screamed again. "Witch," he growled, and the name made me cry. He slapped me across the mouth. The pain astonished me. He doesn't know, I thought, he's still inside it. He can't know. Again he held his hand over my mouth as he pushed on me, dragging me to the end, but I beat his back with the fist of one hand

and felt with my mouth for his fingers. I bit him, listening
to the noise of his howl, and the sound made me happy.
He pulled away, and I sat up, ripping the scarf from my
face and throwing it down on the bed. I tugged at the
blanket and draped it over my shoulders to cover myself
completely. Moving away from him, I withdrew into a
corner of my bed near the window and stared outside,
gazing through the diamond bars of the safety gate into
the airshaft below lit by the moon and distant neon. On
the ground I saw some wayward garbage and stones. Where
did the stones come from? I thought.

Michael grunted, and I turned my head to look at him.
He sat at the edge of the bed, his bare legs apart, his shirt
open. He was crying. I watched him, fascinated by his
shuddering back and the unfamiliar sounds that came from
him—short, uneven blasts of noise. He was ugly in his
misery and it repulsed me. It's difficult to say how long
we remained like that, how long it took before I felt the
turn in myself. It came as a sharp, wrenching sensation in
my gut, and then I pitied him.

He was speaking, the words disguised by sobs. What's
he saying? I thought. I can't make it out. I inched toward
him, taking the blanket with me, and then when I was
very close to him, I put out my hand and hesitated. Finally
I let my fingers rest lightly on his shoulder. The wet stripes
on his cheek struck me as incredible. Fragments of sentences entered my head and then vanished. I opened my
mouth, closed it. Then I whispered, "Why?"

He shook his head, folded his hands in his lap and
rubbed the palms together. I stared at the fingers and saw
the tiny wound where I had drawn blood on one knuckle.

I shifted my gaze from his hand to the bed where the scarf lay still tied on the white sheet. Strange, I thought. Everything is strange.

Michael moved so that he could see himself in the long mirror opposite us. We stared at the reflection. I saw him, saw the soft, pale flesh of his belly, the deep navel and flaccid genitals. I looked away. I had seen it. In the mirror his body appeared as a thing of comic horror, vulnerable, aging, the site of decay.

He saw it too. "Look at me," he said. "I'm an old man, absurd, contemptible."

I moved behind him and studied myself in the glass—the small head and wild hair, the colorless cheeks, the darkness under my eyes, my thin fingers holding the blanket. I let go, and the covering fell to the bed, exposing my naked body, but what I saw then was my mouth. The lips appeared very red and swollen, a lonely sign of blatant sensuality, an advertisement.

Michael seemed transfixed by my reflection.

"Look away, Michael," I whispered to him. "The mirror. Don't stare at me like that."

He met my eyes in the glass, our reflections locked in confrontation. "Can you see it?" he said.

"What?"

"The answer. It's there, in you, on you."

I didn't speak. He looked at me. "No," I said. "It's what you think you see. It's the old thing between us, what you've been trying to say, trying to tell me . . . " I couldn't finish. The vagaries made me tired. Speech was sickening.

Michael continued to look at himself and then at me in the mirror. I moved out of view, covering myself again under the folds of the blanket, and went to open the grate and lift the window. I need air, I thought. Then I breathed it in, cool air that smelled of gasoline, soot, and brick.

"Tonight," he said, "I was someone else." He waited but I said nothing.

"It is"—he paused—"unforgivable."

"You hit me," I said. I stumbled over the phrase, and the emotion returned. I pressed my lips together and closed my eyes.

"I can't believe it." He said this quietly, to himself.

We were silent. Then I moved closer to him and said, "I felt it coming. I almost expected it."

He looked down at his knees.

"Michael," I said, whispering now. "Where did it come from? I don't understand it."

He moved his head sharply upward. "Do you think I can tell you? Do you think I know?"

"You said 'witch.'"

He turned his face to me, his eyes blank.

"Don't you remember? You called me 'witch.'"

His lips moved, saying the word soundlessly, and I stared at him. The room was still dark, except for a light bulb that shone from the outer room. It was enough. I decided not to turn on my lamp.

"Sometimes I feel that what we do and what we say is just a repetition, that's it's all happened before," I said.

"Déjà vu," he said, his voice flat.

"No, not that, not identical—vaguely the same, like we're trapped in a pattern or an idea that we can't give up, that leads us by the nose . . ."

"You want to have a philosophical discussion now?" he said. "My God!" He spoke to the wall.

"No, I just want to understand what happened."

"Iris, we can talk until doomsday and we'll get nowhere."

"I think you wanted a part of me only, a sliver of myself really, and I tried to give you that, but it didn't work. It got all distorted . . ."

Still he didn't turn to look at me. "When I found you, Iris, again, in that bar, you were like a lost boy, a haggard, wild-eyed kid, a little crazy, too. Do you think I've forgotten that? I think about it all the time."

"You saved me from perdition, is that it?"

"No, this might be worse than that. I don't know. What I mean is that I've seen you, really seen you, and what I've seen isn't simple or small. It's complex, ambivalent, mysterious, and it's driven me crazy."

"You're blaming me," I said.

"No, myself. Where are my pants?"

"What?"

"My pants."

"I'm sitting on them. Michael," I said, "I'm sorry."

"Don't say that, Iris. I can't stand it."

I threw him the pants, and he stood up. I looked at the backs of his white legs, at the muscles in his thighs. He pulled on his shorts and then the brown corduroys. He turned toward me, his shirt still open. I switched on the lamp near my bed and looked at him. I noticed the gray hairs growing among the black on his chest. Seeing them brought an ache of tenderness. He was buttoning his shirt. I took his hands and pulled him toward me, but he stiffened and seated himself beside me on the bed.

"I can't accept it, Iris," he said. "Your compassion, forgiveness, whatever. Not now." He nodded to himself. "It's insane to act on every feeling, to be blown God knows where by some momentary compulsion—pity, love, anger, jealousy." He turned his head and frowned at me. "I can see it in your face now, that expression of unbearable kindness, poignancy, goodwill. But it won't last."

"That's all we have, Michael, these moments of great feeling. They disappear and then return. Even saints are sometimes cruel," I added, without quite understanding why. "Don't turn away from me. It doesn't make any sense."

"It makes perfect sense." He stared at the ceiling, lifting his chin, and I saw the line of his neck, the bump of his Adam's apple. Then he let his head fall. "We'll turn ourselves into monsters, don't you see? Or at least I will."

"No. That's wrong."

Michael shook his head and picked up his jacket from the floor.

"Please don't go," I said.

He looked at me but didn't answer.

"You're leaving tomorrow."

I watched him stuff his tie into the pocket of his trousers.

"Stay. Stay tonight."

"No."

He stood up.

"Listen to me," I said. "You can't go without talking to me. We have to resolve this, make it clear."

He walked into the other room and turned around. In the sharp light that hit him from above, he looked dead. His colorless face was a mask.

I went toward him, taking the blanket with me as a cloak, and stopped in front of him. "Don't do this, Michael," I said.

He looked at me steadily. Then he nodded his head, and his mouth moved. For an instant I thought he would cry again, but he didn't.

I put my hands on either side of his face and let the
blanket fall. The breeze from the open window blew over
my skin. "Everything is possible," I said. "Right now, we
can choose. We can decide to begin again." I pressed my
fingers into his cheeks. The words excited me and tears
ran down my face, but there were no sobs. I talked. "You
don't understand, but I do. This is a crisis that can send
us into a new world." I smiled. "It's all right now." I took
my hands away and held them out at my sides. I laughed.
It was true. I was sure of it. My chin was shaking. I cried
and laughed. "There are miracles," I said.

Michael made his eyes small and stared, his face expres-
sionless.

I didn't stop. "It's simple," I said. "One gesture, one sign.
That's all."

Michael didn't move.

I bit my lip. It was finished. Then I turned my head so
as not to see him, and I remembered the ending of "Ra-
punzel." Two of her tears fell into his blind eyes and he
could see. I walked to my closet, found my robe, and put
it on slowly, concentrating on the tie at my waist. I returned
and faced him.

"I'll write," he said.

I nodded. Then I smiled at him. It must have been a
terrible smile, because he shrank from me. He hunched
his shoulders and looked at the floor. With that movement,
he entered the past. When he put on his jacket, kissed me
again, and walked to the door, he was already a memory.
In the doorway he paused to look at me, still as his own
photograph. I must have said goodbye. I don't know. I
recall looking at things in the room after he left—the table
and two chairs, the makeshift sofa, the blanket lying on

the floor—with a kind of detached curiosity. Almost in the same instant, I thought of the suit. When I was a child, I said to myself, I imagined all things were alive. I talked to my toys, my silverware, my shoes. As I locked the door, I was overcome by a desire to resurrect that world.

The summer came, hot and familiar. I bought an air conditioner with my first monthly check. My students in Queens read short stories. They read Melville, Hawthorne, Chekhov, Babel, Kafka. Five days a week, I took the subway and then a bus to Flushing. Late into every night, I corrected grammar and diction, flawed logic and outright nonsense, working long hours to postpone insomnia. Michael didn't write. I thought about him all the time, and when I thought of him, I thought of Klaus. A feeling—guilt, sorrow, depression—had settled beneath my ribs and rarely left me. It grew in every pause: between classes, papers, conversations. When I was alone, that crude lump of emotion was all I felt, and I wanted it gone. A need to purge myself, to tell someone the story started to nag me. I had to talk.

In the middle of July, I taught *The Brutal Boy*. The edition hadn't yet appeared, so I Xeroxed the manuscript and gave it to my class. For two days I harangued my students about the problem of evil. "Who is Klaus?" I finally roared into their surprised faces at the end of the second class. Tina Jaworsky raised her hand. "I don't know, Miss V.," she said. "I think he's a pretty normal kid. He doesn't *do* much." She thought for a moment. "My brother killed his turtle when he was seven, put it in the toilet and flushed. Then he bawled and bawled." The class laughed. I sat down at my desk. "See you tomorrow," I said, ten minutes early.

Krüger's novella provided no clues, no ground for explaining anything. The story was a red herring. It left me empty. Then I decided to return the suit to Ruth and tell her about Klaus and Michael. We met at Tom's Restaurant.

She was there when I arrived, and my old friend looked beautiful to me. Her red hair was pulled back loosely to the top of her head and she wore a simple green sheath of a dress with bronze sandals. Ruth no longer looked like a student.

"How are you, Iris?" she said, her face serious.

"I'm okay, glad to see you, very glad. You look lovely, happy."

"I am," she said. Her gaze was steady.

In her expression I saw an opening, a place to begin. I caught my breath. The suit lay beside me in the dry-cleaning bag.

"I brought your brother's suit," I said.

She looked puzzled and then said, "Oh, that! I'd forgotten all about it. I'm sure he has, too."

"I have to tell you, Ruth . . . " I spoke in a low voice. "I wore it a few times afterward . . ."

Ruth smiled. "That's okay, Iris. You sounded so ominous I thought you were going to say, well, something completely different."

I was silent and looked at her gold earrings. Robert Cohen, I decided, was rich.

"I've done it, Iris," she said.

"Done it?"

"We're married."

"You and the illustrious Mr. Cohen?"

"Oh Iris," she said. Her face fell. "You don't like Robert."

"You're wrong," I said. "I do."

"We did it at the courthouse downtown—fast, with no fuss. We're going to have a party, though, and you're invited. And . . ."

"And you're so happy," I said.

"Yes, but there's more."

I looked at her and smiled. "All right, let's have it."

She stood up and smoothed the material of her dress over her belly. "I'm pregnant."

"Oh Ruth," I said, and then said it again, opening my arms. She hugged me hard, and when she withdrew, I saw her face convulse with emotion.

I couldn't tell her. I knew the reason for my silence was the baby, the fact of her pregnancy, but why her unborn child should have made it impossible for me to speak still eludes me. Before we parted, I said, "I hope it's a girl."

"I really don't care," she said, "as long as it's one or the other." Ruth laughed.

"I know," I said. "But I would like a girl."

"Then I'll wish for a girl," she said, "for you."

Paris resurfaced in the middle of August. I was returning from Queens with fifty uncorrected freshman compositions, and there he was on the stoop of my building in a kelly-green suit, reading a copy of *Interview*.

"Odysseus," he said. "At last you've come home to me."

I grinned at him. "It's been a long time, Penelope."

"Years and years, but I want you to know that I've been saving myself for you."

"How long have you been sitting here?"

"Not long," he said.

"Your timing is inscrutable," I said, looking at the wrinkles around his eyes.

"I'm so glad you think so. How about dinner?"

"I'd be delighted," I said.

Paris took my hand and squeezed it. The heat made the sunlight foggy. I stared at the limestone building across the street. Someone opened a blind in a second-story window. I saw a woman's naked arm and thought of Michael.

Paris waited for me while I showered and changed. He had never seen my apartment, and when I came out of the bedroom, he commented on its austerity.

"That's a euphemism, Paris. The truth is, I'm poor as a church mouse. I'm surprised at your delicacy."

"I'm on my best behavior."

He took me to the Odeon in Tribeca, a shining, crowded place patronized mostly by young people wearing black. They were a preening, elegant bunch who brought to the room a self-consciousness so pronounced it was like action. The restaurant was a chaos of glances cast and then withdrawn, of mental notation—the chic and beautiful admired, the not-so-chic and not-so-beautiful summarily dismissed. With the tiny Paris on my arm, I entered feeling like a giantess in my two-inch heels, hoping my dress didn't betray its bargain basement origins. But once we were at the table, I relaxed. Paris bought champagne and entertained me with quips about people he knew at other tables. "See that woman in the purple jumpsuit, the one with the snub nose? Rich, rich, rich. She owns a gallery, but Daddy made the money trading arms. And over there . . . " He nodded. "That's Rick Hops, the painter. He's gone to seed, paints nothing but oranges. The work stinks. He had his fifteen minutes . . . " I gaped at the various characters one by one. "When are you going to learn, Iris, that ogling is in bad taste?"

"How are you, Paris?" I said.

He stopped smiling. "Not so well." He put his hand to his chest. "Had an attack last night. I could hardly breathe."

"I'm sorry."

"Susan left me Thursday. There's still a lot of her junk in my apartment."

"I didn't know you were living together." I said.

"More or less. Sometimes more, sometimes less."

"It's really over?"

He moved his head in thought. "I've got twenty-seven pairs of her shoes in my closet."

"Twenty-seven?"

"I counted."

"I suppose there are people in the world with twenty-seven pairs of shoes."

Paris stared at his raspberry tart.

"A man I was seeing left me too," I said. This flat statement made me blush. When Paris spoke of Susan, it sounded natural and smooth, hardly private. My reference to Michael nearly choked me.

Paris looked up. "Not Stephen?" he said. "I know Stephen."

"Do you?"

"Yes. He's hanging out with some model, a real twit."

"Oh." Stephen had visited me in the hospital, and I hadn't seen him since. The connection between Paris and Stephen wasn't remarkable. I had heard that Stephen was writing art reviews, and that world was small. Nevertheless, I felt compromised.

"So Stephen mentioned me?" I said.

"He didn't tell me the details of your love life, if that's what you're worried about," he said, "just that you were an old girlfriend." Paris smiled briefly. "He did say that there was some scuttlebutt about you and an older guy, a professor, I think . . ."

I pressed my lips together and stared at Paris. There's no hiding, I thought. We only imagine secrets.

Paris wrinkled his face. "I'm sorry," he said. "Gossip, just gossip. You should hear what they say about me. If it were all true, I'd be sitting in a jar in the Harvard Medical School."

I remembered Ruth and the story of the painter who had committed suicide. An image of the dead man appeared for an instant. Then I saw Michael sitting at the edge of the bed, the knotted scarf lying on the sheet. The din of a hundred conversations filled the room, and close to me was the faint smell of someone sweating.

"Let's blow this Popsicle stand," said Paris as he called the waiter, making a writing gesture with one hand. "Why don't we go to my apartment? It's quiet there."

We took a taxi to Chelsea. Paris said nothing, and I stared out the window. Once he patted my arm. He's kind, I thought. Tonight he's been kind. Paris paid the grim, silent driver and led me into his building and up two flights of stairs. In my recollection, the apartment is all glass— glass tables and walls of green glass blocks and several mirrors—its transparency accentuated by mysterious lights Paris dimmed from a switch on the wall. Nothing was old. Even his books, collected in a large metal case, looked new in their shiny jackets. Paris pointed at a white sofa, sat down opposite me, and poured two brandies.

"I'm sorry I passed on that bit of gossip from Stephen," he said. "I wasn't thinking. Sometimes I run at the mouth. It looks to me like you've been badly hurt."

I looked up at him. "It's not your fault. I'm overly sensitive these days." My eyes were wet and I gulped the brandy.

"It's okay, Iris," he said. "You can tell me. It's okay."

Permission had been granted, and I lunged through the opening like a desperate animal. I spilled the beans. I told him everything: Klaus, Stephen, Michael, the hospital, the night of the blindfold. Sobs invaded my sentences, but I got it out, punctuating all my statements with the moronic refrain "I don't know." When I talked, I didn't look at Paris. I delivered my story to the city on the other side of his large windows, my eyes on its lights and caves of darkness. We were far west, close to the piers and the river. There were periods of intermittent calm when I spoke in a normal voice, struggling to articulate what had happened, and then I would start crying again in earnest, gasping for breath, sniffing and making peculiar little noises. During these intervals, Paris made sympathetic sounds with his tongue, which I took as further license and steered myself back to my confused tale. When I had finally blurted out what I supposed was the last scrap of my confession, I turned to Paris.

He was leaning back in the white chair, holding the snifter with two hands. An invisible ceiling lamp cast a cloud of light over him. I could see the flecks of dust in the beam. He blinked and then yawned. For a fraction of a second the silver fillings in his teeth caught the light. I leaned forward and gripped the arm of the sofa. His face had changed, it seemed to me. He grinned with one corner of his mouth. "I like the part about the cop. I can just see him." Paris laughed.

"It's not funny," I said, staring at him.

"Come on, Klaus," he said, emphasizing the name. "It's a riot."

"No," I said, shaking my head. I moved away from him, inching down the sofa, still looking at his face.

"Iris." He was smiling now. "Have a little perspective, a little humor. You ran around in your Halloween costume for a while. I already know that, and I admit it was a bit weird, but it makes you more interesting. Stephen comes in here somewhere. That disappoints me because, frankly, he's a bore. You're lucky to be rid of him. The whole thing gave you a sick headache and you spent some time in the neuro ward uptown. Then you met what's his name. Let's just call him Gramps. Gramps pushed you around one night and walked out of your life forever. That just about sums it up, doesn't it?"

I stood up. I was dizzy and had to steady myself. "You're a monster," I said to him. My voice was shocked, small. I took a step backward and bumped into the sofa.

"Hey, listen," he said. "I know you feel bad about all this, but if you look at it in another way, it evaporates. It's nothing. I could tell you stories . . . Really, Iris. Sit down."

"I can't believe it. An hour ago you were the sympathetic friend, oozing charity. Who the hell are you now?"

"I don't know why you're so excited. I had a little fun with you, so what?"

"Paris, I trusted you enough to tell you. We've been friends."

He looked at me with blank eyes. "Bullshit," he said without raising his voice. "I've been convenient, a distraction once in a while, but not someone to be taken seriously, hardly a leading man. I'm too short, remember?" He turned the glass in his hand and shrugged.

I felt nauseated. The cognac, I thought. I moved my feet apart to find my balance. "What's your real name?" I said.

He sat in the chair without moving. I've hit a nerve, I said to myself. "The name your parents gave you. What is it?"

He didn't even blink.

"Maybe it's Fred?"

"No, it isn't."

"Arnold," I said. "Arnold's cute. Abe, Alfred, Abner. My God, there are thousands of possibilities. Buddy, Bert, Bertrand, Brian, Billy, Buster, Caleb, Curtis. That's nice." The names soared through my head. "Let's forget the alphabet," I said, my hysteria rising. "Dick, Dickie, Rick, Ricky, Prick." The invective pleased me. "John, Johnny, the John, little John, a John. Oliver, Walter, Allan, George. What was it?"

Paris's smile was placid. "You're crazy." He dipped his finger into his brandy and sucked it. "Give it a rest."

The reflections in the room made me sick. I closed my eyes. "Maybe there's a 'junior' attached to your name. Bob junior, a little Jim. You're a junior, aren't you?" I looked at him. My mouth was quivering uncontrollably.

"Leave it alone," he said. "You're drunk."

I took a breath. My voice was calmer. "Whatever your name is, it must be terrible to be you. Every life can be turned into a bad joke—mine, yours—but why do it? You wanted me to talk. You encouraged it. For what? A jolt of real emotion? An edge? A little power in the big, bad city? Is that it? What possible use do you have for me? I can't do you any good."

"Well said for someone who can't stand up straight," he said. "But you're fooling yourself. You never liked me for my sincerity. I fascinate you. That's the only thing that counts, Iris. You're not as high-and-mighty as you act. There aren't any rules, not really. Who makes them? God? I think you're interested in dirt, in a hint of cruelty. It excites you. Life is the circus, my dear. Why fight it?" Paris opened his arms and waved me toward him.

The room moved. My vision was unstable. "You really mean that, don't you?" I said.

He nodded. "Kiss me," he said, and put a finger to his lips. "Aren't you curious? See how it feels."

"I'm leaving," I said. "I'm leaving right now."

He stood up. The green jacket was a mass of wrinkles. I looked at his silly hairdo with amazement. He put his fingers on my arm. I didn't move. He took my hand and stared at it, rubbing my palm with his thumb. Then he let go, and my arm fell to my side like a piece of wood. "Maybe you're not up to it tonight," he said. "I'll get you a taxi."

"No," I said. I walked toward the door. He shot ahead of me and opened it. In the hallway I turned around and looked over his head into the room. I'm not going to say anything, I thought. Paris had one hand on the doorframe.

"Well, goodbye then," he said. "I'll be in touch."

I looked at his eyes. Then I turned my head very slowly to the right and to the left, a silent no.

Paris moved his hand suddenly from the door and shot it toward me, pushing it over the cloth of my dress between my legs.

My shoulders and my chin trembled. I turned around and took the stairs, gripping the railing as I went down. In the dark street the nausea caught up with me, and I vomited between buildings. For a couple of minutes I stood very still and listened to the sound of my breathing. Then I took off my shoes and ran to the IRT, ran, as they say, like a bat out of hell.